Holly and Ivar

Janet Koops

Brown House Books

For the ones who believe that love moves through the world like winter wind: unseen, but felt in everything.

60
days until
Christmas Eve

HO, HO, HOLD THE ESPRESSO

<u>Holly</u>

She knew better than to have another espresso, but that wasn't going to stop her.

Holly Kringle returned to her desk, liquid gold in hand, and once again analyzed the spreadsheets before her. Production was down from where it was at this point last year, only by a narrow margin, but still, they should be doing better.

Her monthly report was due in a few hours, and she didn't want it to be late. This was her father's first year as Chief Executive Santa, and she didn't want to disappoint him. Some people might think that having your father run the family business made your job easier, but not so. At least not in this family—the Kringle family—with the weight of generations to live up to.

Not that she had much to worry about. Holly was darn good at her job. Running the Northeast Division of America (or NED as everyone called it) was no easy feat. As one of ten regional Santas serving North America, her territory spanned nearly 60 million people, ranging from remote rural towns to the heart of New York City. And she'd managed the region for the past seven years with success.

She had to excel. Her goal was to get her father's job after he retired. The next rung on the ladder was Lead Santa for all of America, though she'd happily take the European division if it meant living in Italy again. After that, Chief Executive Santa. The job title wasn't exactly something she could list on a resume or LinkedIn profile, but within the Kringle network, it was everything.

That's why this production issue had to be her top priority. It was a small blip, but a blip nonetheless. Holly buzzed her assistant with the intercom. "Hi Rita, could you come in here for a moment, please?"

Several minutes later, Rita entered the room. The black-haired, neatly styled woman sat down across from Holly. She wore a black pencil skirt and white blouse embellished with what appeared to be black dots—no, make that tiny snowflakes. Rita had worked at NED for twenty years and knew everything there was to know about the operation. Holly would be lost without her.

"All right, then," Rita said, opening her tablet. "What are we working on?"

"It's the monthly report," Holly began. "I'm not sure if you've noticed, but our production is slightly below where we were at this point last year."

Rita put her glasses on and tapped on her tablet. "Oh yes, I see. It's not too bad, all things considered."

All things considered? Holly laced her fingers together and leaned forward on her desk. "I'm not sure what you mean by that."

"Well," Rita began, removing her reading glasses, "we've had unusually high turnover this year, even for us."

"I guess that's understandable. A lot has changed this year, what with my grandfather retiring and my father taking over."

"I don't think that's the issue," Rita said. "While our turnover rates are lower than in the real world, our division is always the highest in North America at about 2%. Now it's climbed to 3.5%. Unheard of until now. People are transferring to other divisions, but no one is transferring in. Have you looked at last year's employee satisfaction survey?"

"No, I've been too busy."

"Holly, we have the same conversation every year—"

"Yes, yes, yes," Holly interrupted. "I'm well aware of that, but there is so much to do."

Rita sighed. "Nicola and Finn are apprenticing under you. Not only should they be learning that managing human resources is part of being a Santa, you can delegate this to one of them. They're both bright and eager to learn. Teach them and use their talents."

Okay, so maybe Holly had a few control issues on top of her caffeine addiction.

Holly drummed her fingers on her desk, then went for another espresso. "Want one?" she asked Rita.

"No thank you," Rita replied. "And how many is that for you today? I already see three empty cups on your desk."

"That is not your concern." Holly's voice was light, knowing that Rita cared about her. "How many hot cocoas have you had today?"

Rita laughed. "Well, if you want to keep your consumption hidden, at least reuse the cups or put them in the lunchroom dishwasher like I do."

Holly made her espresso, then sat down. "You're right about Nicola and Finn. I've been letting their training slide." She adored her young cousins and knew they would make good Santas one day if that's what they wanted. Nicola had studied engineering and loved the production aspect. Finn, on the other hand, was Mr. Social. Yes, she'd dropped the ball not having Finn focus on HR.

The problem was that she didn't know what the problem was. Her team was compensated fairly, had great healthcare, plenty of time off, a solid retirement plan, and the same benefits as any other division. So why was NED's turnover so high? Give her quantitative data over qualitative any day. How could she fix things if they couldn't be quantified? Just thinking about it made her heart race.

"I don't understand. Our employee benefits outshine those of any other company out there."

"Except that we aren't any other company," Rita said. "Our team members, myself included, are from families that have been with the Kringles for generation after generation. We live in a world hidden away from the rest of society. Our existence is a secret. And yes, while our benefits are wonderful and we can travel across our world or the outside one, being here is a choice. One that is made because of what we do here, the foundation upon which the entire Santa universe rests: the spirit of giving, joy, kindness."

Holly's heart thumped in her chest. "And your point?"

Rita raised her eyebrows and scanned the room.

So what if Holly's office wasn't like her grandfather's old one? He liked Christmas trinkets and traditions and dark wood. Her office was all sharp lines and muted tones, with gray walls, a black desk with chrome legs, and black-and-white photographs of the major cities in her delivery zone. She preferred it that way. No distractions helped her focus. "I like it like this," Holly said.

"I know. You have your own style, and I'm not suggesting you change, but a small touch of Christmas in here wouldn't hurt. A snow globe, a picture, a Santa hat on a hook. Or Christmas cookies in the lunch-room, a tree in the lobby. Do you see where I'm going with this? Our

people need to believe in the magic of Christmas."

"They work for Santa. They don't
have to believe because it's true."

Rita sighed. "Yes, but we're not
just making toys here. Anyone can
make toys. It's about what Santa represents. Forget about magic. I should have said the spirit
of Christmas. Efficiency should not
replace joy."

"So if I wear an ugly Christmas
sweater once a week, all will be
okay? Because if that's what it
takes, I'll do it." She'd add it to
her list. One more thing to do.
Sure, it would be nice to cele-
brate the wonder of Christmas, but
she didn't have the time. Wonder
and joy didn't deliver presents on
time or fix the daily problems that
arose. That was her job. And a job
she had to do well if she wanted to
get promoted.

But would she get promoted if she couldn't solve this morale problem? There was so much to do, and Christmas was only two months away. Two months! Panic gripped her, sending a cold rush through her body. Her heart pounded, and each breath felt harder to catch.

"Are you okay?" Rita asked, standing, her voice full of concern.

"Fine, but could you please get me a glass of water?"

Rita returned quickly and placed the water on Holly's desk. Holly closed her eyes and drank it down. It helped, but not enough.

"I'm paging the medic on call," Rita said.

"No, it's fine. I'll be okay in a minute."

"Holly. Don't be a stubborn fool. I'm getting them." And with that, Rita rushed out of the office.

Alone, Holly attempted to take some deep breaths, but her heart continued to race. Was this a heart attack?

Minutes later, Rita returned, followed by Sanjay the medic along with Nicola and Finn. Great. Now she had an audience.

"Holly, are you okay?" asked Nicola.

"I'm fine," she said.

"I'll be the one to determine that," said Sanjay, motioning to Nicola and Finn to step back.

"Nicola, Finn, let's wait in my office and give Holly some privacy." Rita ushered them out, for which Holly was eternally grateful.

Sanjay nodded and took Holly's vitals.

"Well, the good news is that you're not having a heart attack," Sanjay said. "I do believe, however, that this is the result of stress and lifestyle choices. You were warned about your blood pressure at your last physical."

She was. And she'd done nothing. "Can't I take some medication for it?"

"You can, but you still need some lifestyle changes. Diet, exercise, less stress. They're all contributing factors."

"Thank you, Sanjay. I'll take it into consideration. Perhaps I'll take a vacation after Christmas." Unlikely. What would she even do on a vacation? Lie in the sun?

"Your health is important. It's not something you can put off until you go on holiday. I'll have my office reach out to you for an appointment and we can come up with a health plan."

"Thank you," Holly said. "Now, if you'll excuse me, I have to get back to work. And please tell Rita that I'm fine and don't want to be disturbed for the next hour."

Sanjay nodded and exited her office, leaving her in peace. Needing to clear her mind, she walked to the window and gazed out at the vast wilderness to the north, and then to the east, where the village rooftops dotted the landscape.

Holly prided herself on being well-organized and a problem solver. If she weren't, she'd never have been able to manage NED. Her blood pressure, the production decline, and the HR issues were simply problems she had to fix. Nothing more than that.

ROOTED IN WONDER

<u>Ivar</u>

Most people wouldn't spend their day off at work. But most people didn't work in a forest.

To park ranger Ivar Nilsen, the forest wasn't a workplace. It was a companion. Days spent beneath its canopy restored him. The soft creak of the trees and the whisper of wind reminded him he was part of something larger, older, and endlessly alive.

Unseasonably cold weather meant that last night's storm dropped snow instead of rain, resulting in six inches of fresh snow, the kind that muffled sound and made the air smell of pine resin and cold stone. Sunlight slanted through the branches, scattering light over untouched drifts. All around him stretched a sea of white and ever-green, every trunk frosted, every bough bowed low.

"This is the spot, Al," he said to his husky as they stepped into a small clearing. He shrugged off his pack and pulled out camera gear and a collapsible stool.

Liv, his sister and self-appoint-ed social coordinator, had volun-teered him to take photos for the Christmas Carnival Commit-tee. The images would be printed as greeting cards and sold to raise money for the town's Christmas toy fund.

"You're out there all the time any-way," she'd said. "How hard can it be to take a few pictures?"

It wasn't hard unless you wanted good ones.

He set up the tripod and wait-ed. Al circled twice, then curled into a snowy nest, sighing deeply. Ivar reached down to scratch the husky's head, smiling. Unlike his dog, he wasn't good at sitting still. He needed motion—work, a trail, a project. Anything but idle time, which usually led to his sister pes-tering him about dating again.

That was one reason he spent so much of his free time in the for-est. Out here, the air was clean of questions. He could hike, practice survival skills, or keep refining his endless list of tree identifications. Shrubs and smaller plants might still trip him up, but trees? Those he knew by heart.

And it went beyond species identification. Some trees practically had their own personalities. There was Big Red, a seventy-five-foot red spruce on one of the high ridges, at least three centuries old and towering over the trail like a patient elder. And across the clearing where he sat now stood Lady Grace, a sugar maple whose branches arched like a dancer's arms, graceful even under the weight of snow.

But there was one tree he hadn't found.

It was like searching for a single snowflake in a blizzard. And yet he kept looking. Ever since he'd moved back to Winterwood, after California and all that came with it, he'd been quietly searching. Ten years now. Not obsessively, but faithfully.

A cardinal landed on a dogwood across from him, its scarlet feathers vivid against the pale world. Ivar adjusted the lens and framed the shot carefully before pressing the shutter. The click echoed faintly, causing Al to lift his head.

"Nothing to worry about, buddy," Ivar murmured, giving the dog another scratch. "Go back to your nap."

The husky sighed again, louder this time, and obeyed.

Ivar lingered in the clearing, taking a few more photos of the cardinal, along with a couple of chickadees, and a tangle of snow-coated branches. "I think that's enough," he told Al. "Home or hike?"

Al stood, stretched, and started up the trail that wound deeper into the woods.

"All right," Ivar said, smiling. "A hike it is."

They hadn't gone far when Al froze, one paw lifted, ears pricked forward. Ivar stopped beside him, listening. For a moment, the forest seemed to hold its breath. Then came the sound of something large crashing through the brush. Its steps were heavy, deliberate.

"That's gotta be a moose," Ivar whispered.

They followed the sound, stepping softly until they found a set of fresh moose tracks crossing the path. "By the size of those tracks, my money's on a bull moose," Ivar murmured. "Let's see if we can get a photo."

They followed the tracks another few hundred yards until they spotted the moose standing at a narrow stream, lowering its head to drink. Keeping a respectful distance, Ivar steadied his camera and snapped a few frames.

Then the moose turned.

Its dark eyes met Ivar's, calm but unblinking. Snow drifted from the branches above, but the animal didn't move. For a strange moment, the forest seemed to be watching him. Waiting.

The moose lifted its head, crossed the stream, and paused on the far side.

Ivar's pulse quickened. It was absurd, yet something in the creature's gaze pulled at him—as though it wanted him to follow, as though it could lead him to the tree. The one that had saved his life when he was a boy. The one he'd half-convinced himself he'd imagined.

Yes, it was absolutely absurd.

He blinked and shook his head. The moose turned away, vanishing into the forest. "I'm losing it," he muttered to Al. "Come on, let's get home before I start talking to squirrels."

Thirty minutes later, they reached the trailhead. Ivar opened the truck door, and Al leaped inside, curling immediately onto the seat. He paused for a moment, listening to the soft rush of wind through the pines.

At moments like this, the forest seemed magical. The symmetry of its design, the web of connection, the quiet persistence of life under the snow. If that wasn't magic, what was?

He climbed into the truck and turned the key. The heater coughed to life. Then, as the windshield began to clear, a flash of red caught his eye.

A cardinal landed on the hood.

It hopped up to the windshield, a tiny sprig of evergreen clasped in its beak. For a heartbeat, it looked directly at him. Then it laid the branch gently on the glass and flew off into the trees.

Ivar stared after it.

Ten years ago, on his worst day in California, a cardinal had done the exact same thing, depositing an evergreen sprig on his car as if delivering a message.

He'd packed his things and driven back to Vermont the very next day.

And now, another cardinal. Another sprig. Another message?

He shifted the truck into gear, glancing at the sprig on the windshield. "Right," he murmured. "Definitely losing it." But then he placed the truck in park, rolled down the window, reached out for the sprig, and placed it in his pock-et.

ARE YOU ELFING SERIOUS?

<u>Ivar</u>

With his head still reeling from the cardinal and the branch, Ivar dropped Al off at home, then headed to the Maple Mug Coffee House. He needed to be surrounded by people doing tangible, ordinary things. He needed grounding.

A maple scone wouldn't hurt either.

As soon as he stepped inside, he knew he'd made the right call. Warm air wrapped around him, carrying the scent of espresso, cinnamon, and maple syrup. A jaunty French cafe tune with an accordion floated above the low hum of conversation. A few locals waved. Emma Tremblay was behind the counter, humming along while steaming milk.

"You look like a man in need of sugar. Here," she said, sliding a mug toward him. "I saw you coming from across the street."

"You're the best," he said, taking a sip. "Caffeine first, then sugar. One maple scone, please."

She smiled, plating the scone. "Sit anywhere—I know you and George both like that booth in the corner, and I'm afraid he got there first today."

Sure enough, George Keating occupied the corner seat by the window, hunched over the daily crossword. His pencil hovered in mid-air. "Nine-letter word for stub-born," he muttered as Ivar passed.

"Difficult," Ivar offered.

George grunted, which in George's language meant thank you.

Ivar carried his coffee and scone to a small table near the fire. Mim Daley was pinning new flyers to the community board—announcements layered over lost-and-found notes and photos from last year's Christmas Carnival. One new note caught his eye:

MISSING: one blue fox pattern left mitten. Beside it, someone wrote and my dignity and had doodled a fox smiling beside it.

He smiled, took a bite of his scone, and texted his sister.

Ivar: Got some great photos. I'll send them later.
Liv: [thumbs up emoji]

The scone was perfectly warm, buttery, and sweet enough to remind him there were still simple pleasures in the world.

He'd barely taken another bite when a voice interrupted him.

"Well, hey there, Mr. Park Ranger."

He looked up. Gwen Brooks stood beside his table, coffee in one hand and her phone in the other, radiating the unmistakable energy of Winterwood's number one real estate agent.

"Mind if I join you?" she asked, already pulling out the chair.

"Go ahead," he said, knowing resistance was futile.

"So how've you been?" she asked, settling in.

"Good. Busy."

"Oh, me too—always! Closing a deal this afternoon. First-time buyers. Nervous wrecks, poor things. They're buying the old MacKenzie place on Third. Remember their son, Mac MacKenzie? I'll never understand why his parents named him that. Anyway, he's in Maine now—fishing charters, three kids, can you believe it?"

Ivar nodded politely. "I played hockey with him in high school."

"Of course you did." She took a sip of coffee, eyes sparkling with the thrill of gossip. "Now listen, this is just between us."

He leaned in. "Okay."

"You'll never guess who contacted me. The Hale estate."

He blinked. "Miss Hale's place?"

"Exactly. Her grandniece, a professor in Seattle, inherited it, and she doesn't want it. Wants to sell the whole property, and she's hired me as the agent."

Ivar's stomach dropped. Five thousand acres. Untouched forest bordering state land and interlaced with trails that locals had used for generations.

"Are there any restrictions?" he asked carefully. "Because if a developer buys it—"

Gwen lifted a manicured hand. "Don't know yet. But let's be realistic. No one buys that kind of property to leave it wild. I'm not saying I support development," she added quickly. "My boys ride their bikes through those trails. I love it there too. But I have three teenage boys eating me out of house and home. College in a few years, too. At least for one or two of them. I'm not going to deny that this commission would help me."

He managed a thin smile. "Understandable. But the wrong kind of developer would be disastrous. Maybe the council can do something."

"I'll reach out." She sighed, setting her coffee down. "It's complicated, Ivar. I love the woods too. But the only constant is change, right?"

Before he could answer, she patted his arm, gathered her coat, and leaned close. "I'll keep you posted." Then she was gone, leaving behind the faint scent of expensive perfume and the echo of too many words.

Ivar sat back, watching the snow swirl beyond the window. Around him, the Maple Mug carried on as usual. George muttered over his crossword; Emma filled mugs; Mim straightened the flyers on the board.

So why was he certain his world
was about to change?

32
days until
Christmas Eve

WINTER WHERE?

<u>Holly</u>

Holly checked the time on her new watch. Five minutes early.

For good measure, she tapped the face and checked her heart rate. Normal.

Good. Because she was nervous.

She'd been summoned to her father's office a month before Christmas Eve. Meetings this close to the big night weren't unusual, but a lone summons? Not exactly a good sign. Dad and Aunt Shelly must be concerned about that dip in production on her last report. But she was prepared. They could implement a twenty-four-hour production cycle and streamline shift rotations.

"Ah, there you are, my dear." Her father appeared at the end of the hallway, his voice warm and booming. "Perfect timing as always. Shelly's already inside."

Adam Kringle was no jolly Santa stereotype. Tall, broad-shouldered, and disciplined, he rationed Christmas cookies like currency, allowing himself one each day, and adding ten minutes to his treadmill routine for every extra indulgence. His salt-and-pepper hair was now mostly salt, and his new beard was pure white.

"Hi Dad. Couldn't resist the Santa beard, eh?" she teased.

He chuckled. "I figured I'd try it out. Your mother isn't sold, but she's letting me experiment."

"It's not a requirement," she said. "You don't see Aunt Shelly growing one."

He grinned and scratched his chin. "Touché. Come on in before she finishes the meeting without us."

Shelly Kringle stood by the office sideboard, pouring herself a glass of water from a crystal pitcher. She turned with a bright smile. "Holly! Good to see you, sweetheart."

"You too, Aunt Shelly." Holly took the leather chair across from her father's desk, her eyes flickering around the office. She still found it strange not to see her grandfather there.

Retirement had suited him, though. The last time she'd seen him, he'd looked younger than his eighty-five years, tanned and laughing on his way to another cruise with his new girlfriend—their third that year.

Her father and Shelly took their seats.

Aunt Shelly was Chief Operating Santa, a position she'd held under Grandfather. When he retired, she turned down the top job. It still baffled Holly. Who in their right mind didn't want to be Chief Executive Santa?

But the two made a good team, and her father's transition to the role had gone smoothly. But Adam Kringle had his own style, and the change in leadership was reflected in his office. Gone was Grandfather's cluttered, cozy chaos. Adam had transformed it into something warm and orderly: polished wood panels, plaid cushions, a crackling stone hearth, and a Christmas tree decked in woodland ornaments. Framed photographs of every re-gional workshop lined the wall, while the family's legendary Book of Santa rested in a glass display case beside the first Claus globe.

Adam absentmindedly picked up a snow globe from his desk, gave it a shake, and set it down again.

Holly couldn't wait any longer. "So what's this meeting about?"

Her father and aunt exchanged a look that made her stomach knot.

"We'd like your input on an idea," Adam said carefully.

"Okay…" she said slowly.

He drew a breath. "Shelly and I have been discussing this for a while. We believe the Northeast Division should be divided into two regions."

Holly blinked. "What?" She laughed, waiting for him to smile back. He didn't. "This is a joke, right?"

"No," Shelly said gently. "It's time."

"And what does Leif have to say about this?" she demanded. Her cousin was the American Lead Santa. "Shouldn't he be here?"

"Unfortunately, Leif's come down with the flu," Shelly said, "but this was his suggestion originally."

"So this is about the production dip." Holly straightened. "I already have a plan."

Adam raised a hand. "It's not about the report, Hol. We've been considering this for some time."

"For how long? Is that why I'm training Nicola and Finn? Because they're going to be my replacements?" Her pulse spiked, and her watch helpfully beeped to confirm it.

"Not replacements," Shelly said quickly. "Apprentices. But yes, easing the workload is part of it.
The job satisfaction numbers and turnover rates can't be ignored. Dividing the region and building a new workshop will help relieve the strain."

Adam took a sip of water and leaned forward. "But more than numbers and dips in production, we're worried about you."

Holly froze. "Me?"

"You're overworked," he said simply. "You push yourself too hard."

"What did Rita tell you? Because I'm monitoring it." She held up her wrist. "See? Heart rate. Sleep tracker. Totally under control." The watch beeped again, traitorously.

"Rita didn't tell us anything," Adam said. "But I read the department logs. When a medic gets called to your office, it's hard not to notice. We'd never pry into your records, but it's obvious you're burning out. Honey, you look exhausted. There's more to being a Santa than production numbers."

Was there, though? For Holly, being a Santa was everything. Her goal. Her identity. Her legacy. She didn't need hobbies or a social life; she had purpose. And that was enough.

"So," she said tightly, "are you firing me?"

Adam laughed his deep, familiar Santa laugh. "Firing you? Of course not! We just want you to take a break."

"But you're dividing my region."

"Likely, yes," Shelly said, "but we'd never do it without your input. For now, though, we're insisting you take some time off."

"A vacation?" Holly repeated, incredulous. "Now? A month before Christmas?"

"Think of it as a working holiday," Shelly said, cheerful as ever. "A change of scenery. It might do you good."

Adam reached into a drawer and pulled out a folder. "If we're building a new workshop, we need a new location and a new power source. One of our scouts located a potential Yule vein in a Vermont forest. The property's just gone up for sale." He slid the folder across the desk to Holly. "So, we'd like you to assess the site and determine whether the Yule vein is powerful enough for our needs."

Holly opened the folder. "And this can't wait?"

"No," Adam replied. "The property has already been on the market for a few weeks now. If this has what we need, we'll have to move fast."

She took a moment to scan the report. "Winterwood?"

"That's the nearest town," Shelly said.

"You're not planning another Mistletoe setup, are you?" Holly asked. Her brother Martin had established his workshop right in town, hidden in plain sight.

Adam shook his head. "No. This will be one of our traditional hidden villages."

The room fell quiet except for the soft ticking of the clocks on the wall.

The thought of dividing her region still stung, but neither her aunt nor her father seemed angry, so this wasn't a demotion. Maybe it was a test to assess her adaptability, her leadership, her readiness for the next step. If that was the case, then she'd do it, and she'd do it better than anyone else.

Fine, then. She'd go to Winter-where-ever, find the Yule vein, make her report, and get back to NED with a few weeks left before Christmas Eve. How hard could it be?

"All right," she told them. "Consider it done. When do I leave?"

26
days until
Christmas Eve

SANTA-MENTAL VALUE

<u>Holly</u>

One week later, Holly paced across her kitchen, reviewing her list for at least the tenth time. Warm clothes. Toiletries. Hiking boots. Laptop. Tablet.

She had a nagging sensation that she was forgetting something, but what?

Crossing into her bedroom, she reached for the suitcase stored on the top closet shelf. Dust puffed down in a soft gray cloud. Right. It had been a while. She rarely traveled overnight. The ability to travel somewhere in an instant was one of the perks of Santa magic.

But that's not how she planned to travel to Winterwood, so she wiped the case off and set it on the bed.

She checked off items under the Warm Clothes category: jeans. hiking pants, long johns (because she really hated being cold), long-sleeve shirts, sweaters, more sweaters, wool socks, and flannel pajamas.

How much of each? What if the trip took longer than a few days? If she were delayed in Winterwood with Christmas so close, extra clothes would be the least of her worries, but she added extras anyway.

Rolling her clothes with precision, she organized them neatly inside the bag. Then frowned. Too many sweaters. She climbed onto the bed, sat on the suitcase, and pressed down. The zipper refused to cooperate.

"Of course," she muttered.

She'd need the matching carry-on. Reaching for the closet shelf again, she hit the edge of the bag with her fingertips, knocking it farther back. With a sigh, she retrieved the stepstool from the garage, climbed up, and peered over the top shelf.

And froze.

There it was.

Not the carry-on, though it was there too, but her broomstick, tucked neatly behind it.

For a long moment, she simply stared at it. How many years had it sat there, untouched? Six at least. She'd placed it there soon after taking over NED and never thought about it again.

At one time, it had meant the world to her.

She reached out, fingertips brushing the chipped and rutted wooden handle. A faint hum rippled through her hand. The room stilled, and suddenly she was somewhere else.

Sunlight spilled over a long wooden table. The scent of basil, roasted tomatoes, and warm bread filled the air. Laughter and music drifted around her like a breeze.

It was the end of her apprenticeship in Italy, her farewell banquet. Everyone had gathered, the Santa and Befana branches of the family together, their differences forgotten over shared tiramisu and espresso.

As the evening drew to a close, La Befana herself rose from her chair. Conversation quieted as her kind, sharp eyes fixed on Holly with such intensity, it was as if she could see straight into her soul. Then, with deliberate grace, she lifted the broomstick and held it out. Holly accepted it with trembling hands and a rush of gratitude.

In Italy, La Befana would fly on her broomstick, delivering sweets to good children and sugar coal to the bad ones, so that even the naughty children got something in the end, signifying that even past mistakes can lead to fresh starts.

Unlike Santa's Christmas Eve delivery, La Befana arrived on Epiphany Eve, sweeping away the old year with her broom and making way for the new one. Closure and renewal. Magic could transform, not only deliver. That fascinated Holly and was the reason she'd chosen to apprentice there.

But reality had a way of intruding. In California, she'd spent two years as an assistant Santa, sneaking midnight flights over San Francisco. When she transferred to NED, she'd taken it out only once. On her first night there, she'd flown through New York City, weaving through skyscrapers and shadows. After that, the workload piled up, and the broom had slowly moved from her office corner to her home, and finally to the top shelf of her closet.

Now it looked more like a relic than a piece of her own heart.

Her fingers tingled from its touch. And for a fleeting second, she wondered if she could fly to Winterwood. It would be efficient after all.

But she pictured herself arriving at the Winterwood Inn, hair windblown, luggage nonexistent, trying to explain to a polite innkeeper why she hadn't come by car.

Not practical. And definitely not discreet. No, the broom would stay where it was.

She dusted the carry-on, packed the remaining clothes, and zipped it up without further incident. Within ten minutes, everything was ready.

If she woke at six, she'd be on the road by seven and reach Winter-wood by nightfall.

And as she double-checked her re-minders one last time, the broom-stick was quickly forgotten.

She was getting ready for bed when her phone buzzed with a text.

Rita: Don't forget to pack your won-der along with your computer.

And try to have some fun. I hear Vermont forests can be quite spectacular this time of year. I'd say, call me if you need me, but I know you'll be in touch. Daily. Probably hourly. X O

Holly smiled despite herself. Rita's sentimentality was both endearing and baffling. Wonder wasn't something you packed like an extra sweater. It either existed or it didn't. And right now, with her division potentially being split apart, wonder was the least of her concerns.

STUMPED FOR WORDS

<u>Ivar</u>

"Mom, can we be excused?" Wyatt asked.

"Sure," Liv said.

Wyatt elbowed his younger brother, and both boys carried their plates into the kitchen.

"Put them in the dishwasher, not on it," Liv called after them.

"Yes, Mom," came the chorus from the other room.

Ivar grinned. "So your sign above the dishwasher that says 'This is not the dishwasher' didn't work?"

Liv sighed. "Nope. They pushed it out of the way to set their plates on top. I mean, how hard is it once you're already standing in front of it? Gavin was the same way. I guess it's genetic."

Ivar chuckled, glad to hear his brother-in-law's name spoken with warmth rather than sorrow. In the months after Gavin's passing, Liv couldn't even mention him without tears. Now, more often than not, the memories came with laughter instead of pain.

"You're doing a good job with them," he said quietly.

She smiled, soft and sure. "They keep me busy. That helps."

He nodded, then gestured toward the window where snow was

falling steadily. "How's business? The no-vacancy sign has been glowing for weeks."

"Oh, it's great. The Thanksgiving crowd checks out this weekend, but I'm nearly full for next week, too." She leaned across the table, lowering her voice conspiratorially. "Someone made a reservation last night. At first, I thought it was a prank. You'll never guess her name."

"Seymore Butts?"

"Not quite." Liv's grin widened. "It's more seasonal: Holly Kringle."

Ivar laughed. "You're kidding."

Liv placed her hand on her heart. "I swear I'm not. That was the name on the credit card she gave me. Apparently, she gets questioned about it all the time."

"I bet. Poor woman. That's a tough name to live with."

"Well, whatever her name is, I'm just happy she booked for the week," Liv said, gathering plates. "Want to know why she's here?"

"Does it matter? You're going to tell me anyway."

"She's here to look at the Hale land," Liv said, and Ivar could feel her gauging his reaction. "Her family's interested in purchasing it, and she's here to assess its suitability."

Ivar's stomach tightened. The Hale property. Gwen had told him there'd been no serious inquiries yet. "What does she want it for?"

"She didn't say, and I didn't ask. But this is where it gets interesting. She's not interested in the house, just the forest. And since she mentioned needing someone to show her around, I—"

"Oh, no." Ivar pushed his chair back. "Don't say it."

"Oh yes," Liv said, mischief glinting in her eyes. "Who knows the forest better than you?"

"I have a job."

"Nice try. Your vacation is next week. It's on my calendar."

"Not anymore," he muttered. "I'll reschedule."

"Ivar, come on. What's the big deal?"

"You know how I feel about that sale," he said. "Why should I help someone who might destroy the land I've spent years protecting?"

"Because it's going to happen whether you like it or not," Liv said evenly. "And we were raised to look for the good in people first. Maybe she's not what you think."

He rubbed the back of his neck. "People aren't always what they seem, either. All it takes is the right investor and a little paperwork. Forest or not, if the money's there, they'll build whatever they want."

"Cynical much?"

"Realistic."

Liv folded her arms. "Right. One of these days, you're going to have to stop letting the past—"

He held up a hand. "Stop right there. We're not doing this."

Her expression softened. "I didn't mean—"

"I know." He rose and began clearing the table. "Thanks for dinner. It was great."

"Don't you dare leave without leftovers," she said, following him into the kitchen. "Al loves my lasagna almost as much as you do."

They worked side by side in easy silence, the clatter of dishes filling the comfortable quiet. When the kitchen was spotless, Ivar called to Al, who was sprawled on the rug by the fireplace. Al stretched, shook, and followed him out into the cold.

"Can you at least consider showing her around?" Liv asked from the doorway, arms crossed but smiling.

Ivar sighed. "I'll think about it."

The truck door groaned as he opened it, and Al jumped inside with a thump. The dog pressed his nose to the window, tapping his paw against the door.

"I'm only opening it a bit," Ivar said, starting the engine and then lowering Al's window an inch.

Now Al's nose was pressed into the gap, and he made a sad little whining sound.

"Oh, fine," Ivar said, lowering the window so Al's head could pop out the side.

Snow swirled into the cab as much as under the headlights as they drove toward the cabin. "I could make you ride in the truck bed, you know," Ivar said. "You're lucky I'm a soft touch."

The only reply was the happy rhythm of Al's tail against the seat.

When they reached the cabin, Ivar turned off the ignition but didn't move right away. "All right, counselor," he said to the dog. "I've been thinking I should go with this Holly Kringle after all. That way I can find out what she plans for the land, and if it's bad news, maybe I can steer her in another direction. Forewarned is forearmed, right?"

Al tilted his head, listening, or pretending to.

"Good talk," Ivar said. "Glad we're on the same page."

Al gave a low, approving growl that almost sounded like agreement.

Ivar grinned and stepped out into the darkness. "It's settled," he told the night. "I'll be Holly Kringle's guide to the wilderness."

25
days until
Christmas Eve

ROOM WITH A BROOM

<u>Holly</u>

The drive to Winterwood had been surprisingly pleasant and almost restful.

Because it was technically a work trip, Holly didn't feel the usual guilt that crept in whenever she wasn't being productive. She'd munched on road-trip snacks, listened to an audiobook about leadership psy-chology, and watched the land-scape transform from city skylines to wide open highways, then to the winding, snow-dusted roads of Vermont.

Now it was dark, and as she turned onto the long, lantern-lined drive, she found herself driving straight into a Christmas card.

The Winterwood Inn glowed against the night, its white clapboard siding shining beneath strings of golden lights. Two towering Christmas trees flanked the front steps, each wrapped in garland and silver ribbon. Evergreen boughs framed the veranda railings, and the path from the parking area was lit by small glass lanterns sunk into snowbanks.

Grandfather would love it here, she thought, and made a mental note to send him a photo. He'd probably add it to his "must-visit" list of festive destinations.

Holly parked her car, grabbed her purse, and headed up the steps. The door opened easily, and the scent of pine and wood polish greeted her while the wide-plank floorboards creaked underfoot.

At the reception desk, a blond woman stepped out from the adjoining office, a clipboard in hand. Her smile was as warm as the candle-style sconces glowing along the walls.

"You must be Holly Kringle," she said. "Welcome to the Winterwood Inn. I'm Liv Nilsen. I hope the drive treated you kindly."

"It did, thank you." Holly managed a small smile, though fatigue was catching up with her. A bed, or perhaps a bath in a soaker tub, sounded perfect.

"Well, we've got you in Room Four, the Juniper Room." Liv slid a brass key across the counter. "Up the stairs, first door on your left. Breakfast starts at six, but if you're an early riser, we always have coffee and pastries out here in the lobby. There's also the Maple Mug Coffee House down the street. Opens at seven."

"Perfect," Holly said, taking the key.

"The dining room's still open for another fifteen minutes if you'd like a proper meal," Liv added. "Or the Sugarhouse Brewery is right across the street. They serve good food and great beer."

Holly opened her mouth to decline just as the dining-room doors swung open, releasing the mouth-watering aroma of something rich and savory. Her stomach betrayed her with a loud growl.

Liv grinned. "That settles it. Come have a quick dinner with me on the house. Consider it a welcome to Winterwood."

"Oh, I couldn't."

"You absolutely could," Liv said cheerfully, already leading the way. "It's Christmas, after all. Let me play hostess properly."

Holly hesitated, then sighed. "All right. Thank you."

"This should get me onto Santa's nice list," Liv teased as they stepped into the dining room.

Holly's mouth dropped open. Surely the woman was joking.

Liv's expression softened. "Sorry. I imagine you hear that sort of thing all the time."

"It's fine," Holly said quickly, following her to a corner table near the fire.

The room was a study in warmth: honey-colored wainscoting, a stone fireplace flickering in the corner, stockings hung neatly along the mantel. The wallpaper above the paneling was patterned with faint gold pine boughs, catching the firelight just enough to shimmer. Garland twined along the ceiling beams, and each table held a candle ringed with small poinsettias. The chair creaked companionably as she sat.

"I'll tell the kitchen we're here," Liv said, disappearing through a swinging door. She returned a moment later with menus. "I already know what I'm having—the maple-braised beef stew. It's been simmering since breakfast."

"So that's what smells so good," Holly said, letting out a long breath as her shoulders eased. The place was so cozy, even she couldn't help but relax.

"Yup. Tempted me all day. The Vermont cheddar mac and cheese is also excellent. If you're vegan, there's a roasted squash risotto."

"You had me at stew," Holly said.

Liv laughed, a bright sound that filled the space.

When the waitress left with their orders, Liv chatted easily, asking about the trip, where Holly was from, if she needed anything for her stay. Holly kept her answers brief, polite, and vague. The fewer details, the better.

"So," Liv said, "you're here to look at the Hale land, right?"

Holly nodded. "Yes."

"Do you have plans for the land?"

We want to build a secret Santa village fueled by a magical power vein beneath the forest.

"Nothing concrete," she said. "We see it as an investment."

Liv nodded, apparently satisfied. "That land's beautiful. A lot of us grew up hiking there. Miss Hale never minded. Feels strange, thinking of it changing hands."

Before Holly could respond, the waitress returned, setting steaming bowls of stew in front of them, along with a plate of warm, crusty bread.

The smell of rich beef, roasted vegetables, and the faint sweetness of maple was intoxicating. Holly took a bite and almost groaned. The beef melted on her tongue, and the carrots and parsnips were soft and sweet.

"I think I'm in love," she said before she could stop herself.

Liv laughed. "That's why it's my favorite."

They were finishing the last of the bread when the dining room doors opened again. Two boys burst in, both flushed from the cold. A tall man followed at a calmer pace, shaking snow from his jacket. He was an inch or two over six feet, with blond hair poking out from under his beanie and glacier-blue eyes that seemed to hold a thousand secrets. Holly blinked. Where had that come from?

"Mom, we're back from hockey," the younger boy announced.

"I can see that," Liv said, smiling. "I'm just finishing here. Homework, then bed. And thank Uncle Ivar."

The boys chorused their thanks and bounded away.

"Sorry for the interruption," Liv said, turning back to Holly. "That was my crew. We live behind the inn in a small house, so we're close, but not too close." She grinned. "Otherwise they'd eat through my profits."

Liv turned to the man still standing nearby. "Join us. This is Ivar, my brother. He's a park ranger. I believe I mentioned on the phone that he might be a good guide while you're exploring the Hale property."

Holly tried not to stare at those icy blue eyes, so she focused on the rest of him instead. With worn jeans, a plaid flannel shirt, and a brown barn jacket, he practically defined Vermont.

And yet, he looked like he'd rather be anywhere else at the moment.

"I don't want to impose on anyone," she said quickly.

"Nonsense," Liv said. "Ivar knows the forest better than anyone."

"Nice to meet you, Holly." Ivar's voice was low and steady. "What exactly does your family want it for?"

"An investment," she said.

"In a forest?" His brow furrowed. "You're not planning to log or build?"

"Not log, but maybe someday—"

"Sorry," Liv cut in. "He's protective of the land. It's been a big topic in town."

"I understand," Holly said. "We're simply exploring some options right now."

"I'm free tomorrow, if you are," Ivar said, only a hint of resignation slipping through as he glanced at his sister. "We can start early."

It didn't sound quite like an offer. Holly had the distinct impression he'd rather face a blizzard than play tour guide, but starting tomorrow instead of wasting the day finding someone else was fine with her.

"Okay," she agreed. "That would be great."

"Great," he echoed. "If you'll excuse me."

He turned to go, but Liv's hand shot out to stop him. "Can you grab Holly's luggage from her car? I noticed she didn't have any when she checked in."

"Oh, that's not necessary," Holly said.

"Nonsense," Liv replied. "It's cold out. Let him."

Reluctantly, Holly handed over her key. "It's the black Prius."

Ivar nodded, gave his sister a look that translated to you owe me, and disappeared through the door.

Holly stood, smiling. "Thank you again for dinner. I'm going to sleep like a log."

"My pleasure," Liv said, following her into the lobby. "Welcome to Winterwood, Holly. I have a feeling you're going to like it here."

Moments later, Ivar returned. A suitcase in each hand, and something tucked under an arm. He placed the suitcases on the floor, then reached for the remaining item. It was long and oddly wrapped. The end of a wooden handle peeked through the fabric.

Holly's watch began to beep.

"I'll take that," she said, reaching for the broomstick. Their fingers brushed as she took it, and in that brief moment of contact, the broom seemed to vibrate ever so slightly between them. A subtle tremor traveled up her arm like a current.

A warmth spread through her fingers where their hands had

touched, despite the chill clinging to his skin from the outdoors. Ivar's eyes widened almost imperceptibly, and for a heartbeat, his expression shifted from guarded to startled.

Had he felt it too? The strange pulse of... something... that had passed between them?

She pulled the broom away, pulse racing, watch beeping.

Ivar cleared his throat. "You're traveling with a broom?"

Holly swallowed, trying to ignore the lingering warmth in her fingertips. "It's for sweeping up bad first impressions."

When Holly opened the door to her room, she could have been stepping into her grandfather's house.

A four-poster bed stood draped in a patchwork quilt of deep reds and forest greens. A small stone fireplace waited with kindling stacked beside it, and on the mantel sat a mug, a packet of peppermint cocoa mix, and a sprig of holly.

It was cozy.

Too cozy, maybe.

Holly set her purse on the dresser and turned her attention to the broom, leaning it against the wall, and staring at it as if it might start explaining itself.

"What are you doing here?" she asked under her breath. "I left you in the closet."

The broom, unsurprisingly, said nothing.

She crossed her arms. "Don't look at me like that. I didn't pack you."

The broom remained stoic, wooden, unbothered. "Rita would say this is a metaphor," she muttered. "Reconnecting with my past, or something hokey like that."

The corner of the bed sank as she perched on the edge, staring at the broom. It was then she recalled the rest of the scene from her farewell banquet in Italy. La Befana had approached her and held out the broom. When Holly grasped the handle, La Befana laid her hands over hers, moving closer, her voice low. "Our brooms are carved from the Tree of the Ancients. Passed from mother to daughter, never beyond the family line. But this one... it wants you. Don't ask why. Not yet. When the time comes, it will guide you to the truth your heart has forgotten."

Holly dismissed the memory with a shake of her head. The broom was a means of transportation. A way to get the job done.

And yet, the broom was in the room with her. She was talking to it, and even stranger, the broom wanted to be there.

Holly huffed out a laugh and stood, unzipping her suitcase. "Fine. Whatever. But if you open the mini-bar, you're kindling."

24
days until
Christmas Eve

FIR BETTER OR WORSE

<u>Ivar</u>

Kisses were a nice way to wake up. Dog kisses? Not so much.

Ivar opened his eyes to find Al's enormous amber ones staring back at him from inches away, tail thumping with impatience.

"Morning to you too," he muttered.

Al gave a short, huffy bark, meaning, let's go then.

Ivar groaned, pushed back the covers, and let him out into the yard. Cold air swept in as Al bounded through the snow, leaving a flurry of paw prints in his wake. When the dog was done, he tapped at the door to be let back in and then jumped straight onto the bed, scattering wet paw prints across the clean sheets.

"I guess I'm up," Ivar muttered, sighing.

Al curled into a ball and promptly went back to sleep.

If only he could do that too. It wasn't that he was dreading the day.

Okay, he was absolutely dreading the day.

Spending his time off with someone who might limit access to the forest wasn't his idea of a good time. And that was the best-case scenario. Worst case, Holly Kringle and her mysterious "family business" could tear apart the land he loved most.

While his coffee brewed, he stood by the window and stared out at the pond behind the house. A record-breaking cold month meant that the pond was frozen solid now, a smooth white sheet framed by spruce and birch. The trees stood dusted with snow, silent and watchful.

The possibility of losing all those trees made his stomach twist. What if one of those cut down was his tree?

He shivered.

Despite everything, he knew he had to go. It was the only way to find out what Holly Kringle planned.

He packed his bag with the first aid kit, water, and safety equipment, then attached the snowmobile trailer to his truck. He also threw in two pairs of snowshoes, walking sticks, and extra gloves. If she was going to wander the Hale property, he wasn't letting her freeze or fall through a snowdrift.

"Let's go, Al."

The husky jumped up, eager as ever.

They reached the Winterwood Inn fifteen minutes early, which gave Ivar just enough time to sneak a cinnamon bun from the breakfast buffet. The inn's chef baked them fresh every morning, and they were always warm, gooey, and heavy with icing. Exactly the kind of fuel he needed for a long day in the cold.

He was halfway through licking frosting off his fingers when his sister appeared, hands on her hips.

"You are going to pay for that, right?"

"Of course," Ivar said, wiping icing from his chin. "Right after you pay me for fixing your leaky bathroom faucet."

"Uh-huh." Liv arched an eyebrow.

He shrugged. "I'm early."

"That's a first."

Before he could reply, footsteps sounded on the stairs. Holly's dark hair and warm brown eyes were almost completely hidden beneath her scarf and hat. When she stepped off the stairs, wrapped in enough layers to summit Everest, he had to bite back a smile.

"Good morning," she said brightly, then caught his expression. "What?"

"Nothing."

"I can tell by your face it's not nothing."

He tried unsuccessfully to hide his grin. "We're in Vermont, not the Yukon."

"I know," she said, sounding mildly offended. "But I don't like being cold."

"That's fair," he said. "But you'll need to be able to bend your arms and legs at some point."

Holly's eyes narrowed and were cold enough to freeze his coffee.

"I made arrangements with Liv," he said quickly, still smiling. "You can borrow her snowmobile suit. Trust me. You won't be cold in that."

As if on cue, Liv emerged from the back hallway, holding up a teal snowsuit.

"Here you go," she said, grinning. "Guaranteed to keep you toasty. It's practically magic."

"Thank you," Holly said. "I guess it wouldn't hurt to lose a few layers." She clutched the suit and headed back up the stairs. "Give me two minutes."

"I'll warm up the truck," Ivar said, slipping on his gloves. "Liv, Al's in your office, by the way, already asleep."

"I'll keep him company. You sure you're good with this?"

"Define 'good,'" Ivar said.

She smirked. "Define 'grumpy.'"

He shot her a look, but there was no heat behind it.

"Be nice," she added. "She seems nervous."

"Yeah, well, she's not the only one," he said, tugging his hat down over his ears.

Liv laughed softly as he headed for the door. "Be careful out there, Ranger."

"Always am," he said.

Outside, Ivar crossed to his truck, wondering what bothered him more—the idea of losing the forest or his growing curiosity about a woman with an odd name who traveled with a broom.

What was up with that thing? His fingers tingled slightly at the memory of their hands brushing over its handle. That strange vibration. He flexed his hand absently, trying to dismiss the sensation as either static electricity or the cold.

He allowed himself a big stretch before climbing into the truck, hoping to clear his head. Brooms don't vibrate. He was imagining things. Probably due to his stress over the forest's future.

What else could it be?

ONE HORSE OPEN SNOWMOBILE

<u>Holly</u>

Holly stared at the windshield crack stretching like a jagged fault line across the glass. Snowflakes landed and melted on the edges, refracting tiny shards of light. The longer she stared at it, the more it seemed to creep outward, making it impossible to ignore.

Ridiculous that it bothered her so much. But there it was, right in front of her face, spreading.

"What happened to your windshield?" The words escaped before she could stop them.

Ivar's brow furrowed. "Sorry?"

"Your windshield," she clarified, wincing inwardly. Her tone came out sharper than intended. "The crack. It's spreading."

He glanced at it, then back at the road. "A rock hit it on the highway. Before I could get it fixed, it ran."

"How long are you going to wait?" Another wince. "I mean, is it safe to drive with it like that? Can you even get it fixed around here?"

His mouth twitched, not quite a smile. "We don't have a specialized glass shop in town. The garage ordered a replacement, but it takes a while. I was supposed to take it in today." He paused, giving her a quick glance. "Then my schedule changed."

Holly's cheeks warmed. Right. Because of her. "Oh. Well, thank you."

"It's fine. I'll drop it off when we get back, and it will be fixed by morning."

She nodded and stared out the window, feeling small. "I wasn't trying to criticize. I just... well, I'm a bit of a perfectionist. My sister calls me—" She almost said 'Spreadsheet Santa.' "Spreadsheet Holly. Others agree with her. Hence, this trip."

Ivar cut her a sidelong glance. "You were told to take a break."

"Something like that."

"So you like this kind of thing? Forests, snow, hiking?"

She gave a small laugh. "Not lately. I used to. As a kid."

"What changed?"

"Work. Priorities."

"But if you used to love it then…"

"I used to love a lot of things," she said softer than intended.

He let it drop, and for a moment the only sound was the hum of the engine.

"I'm also cutting back on caffeine," she blurted, still embarrassed over the cracked-windshield interrogation. "So if I sound cranky, that's why. I promised my assistant I'd use this trip to quit espressos. Out of the office and away from the machine, it seemed doable. In theory."

Ivar's mouth curved. "I never noticed. But if I'd known sooner, I'd have filled the thermos with something other than coffee."

"It's fine. Regular coffee's fine. So are lattes. Just not those strong, flavorful shots of liquid gold."

He chuckled.

"What?"

"You really do have a problem, don't you?"

"Perhaps. Yes." She cleared her throat, eager to move on. "So, are there a lot of trails on this property?"

"Plenty. The Hale family never posted the land. The town owns about a hundred acres of forest. State forest borders it to the south, and the Hale land runs along the west and north edges. Trails weave through it all. People bike, ski, snowshoe. There's something for every season."

"You make it sound idyllic."

"It is. That's why everyone's worried about the sale."

"I imagine so." She shifted in her seat. Too bad she couldn't tell him the truth. Even if her family built a site, no one would ever see it, and most of the forest would remain open to the town.

The truck bounced as they turned down a narrow, snow-packed road.

When they finally stopped, Holly stretched, easing the stiffness from her legs. "I should be clear about my objectives today. I need to assess the property systematically." She tapped her tablet. "I've developed a grid pattern for our exploration that should maximize efficiency. Just tell me our coordinates so I can plot them on the map."

Ivar's jaw tightened slightly. "With all due respect, that's not how this forest works. The land has its own logic. Following game trails and water systems will show you more than any grid pattern."

"I appreciate the input." She pulled up her spreadsheet. "But if we stick to my schedule, we—"

"Will miss everything that matters." His voice stayed quiet but firm. "You hired me as a guide because I know this land. Let me actually guide you."

She took in the wilderness beyond the truck. This was so far out of her wheelhouse, it was tempting to turn around and walk away. All her talk about spreadsheets and grids and coordinates was exactly that—talk. She had no idea how to search a forest, so if this park ranger wanted to do it his way, fine. As long as she could get it done and get back to NED.

"Okay. We'll do it your way."

He replied with a curt nod, then exited the truck. If her quick agreement surprised him, he had the courtesy not to show it.

With a deep breath, she opened the door and hopped out into the snow. Despite the chilling wind, the snowsuit kept her toasty warm. It would be heavenly on the Christmas Eve run. "I might have to get one of these snowsuits."

"Eli at Evergreen Outfitters sells them. I'll introduce you later."

"Do you think they come in red and white?"

That got a laugh out of Ivar. "Holly Kringle, you are surprisingly funny. Now here, take this." He handed her a helmet. "Ready to get going?"

"As I'll ever be."

"Bluetooth's on. You'll hear me in your headset."

As they mounted the snowmobile, Holly clutched her tablet protectively inside her jacket. This should be straightforward. Explore the forest systematically and make an assessment. Not that she was sure how that was supposed to happen. She had no equipment to measure Yule line power, although she was pretty sure some existed. How else would the scouts predict potential areas?

The only guidance she'd received was one of her father's classic cryptic messages: Magic doesn't shout, my girl. It whispers, and only to those willing to listen.

Seriously. What did that even mean? At least he'd given her a map.

"The route I've planned takes us to Wolf Ridge first." Ivar's voice came through clear in her helmet. "It gives the best overview of the property."

"Sure. Just let me know the coordinates later, so I can check it off my map."

"What would make it easier would be if you told me what you wanted to do with the land. That would provide me with some direction."

Holly hesitated. "It's hard to explain, but I'm looking for the right kind of vibe."

"Vibe?"

"Yes, that's correct." It sounded utterly ridiculous. It was utterly ridiculous, but her father had insisted this was the tradition. A Kringle skill that needed honing once in a while. This convinced Holly that it was part of her evaluation for promotion. She had to find the Yule vein, and if that meant Ivar taking her through every inch of the forest, so be it.

The snowmobile ride was exhilarating. At least for the first hour. By the third, Holly's muscles felt like overworked taffy. When they finally stopped, she climbed off stiffly, stretching until her joints popped.

"For sitting still, I feel like I've run a marathon," she groaned.

"You'll feel it tomorrow," Ivar said. "The hot tub helps. Ask Liv about it."

"I plan to test that theory extensively, so long as that outfitting store you mentioned sells bathing suits."

As she finished stepping out of the snowsuit, her stomach growled loud enough for Ivar to hear from several steps away. Great. Now both Nilsen siblings had heard it. Hopefully, there weren't more in town.

She flashed him an embarrassed smile and retrieved an energy bar from her bag. "Want one?"

He shook his head. "Get in the truck. I know a better option."

"I'm fine."

"Humor me. My sister will kill me if I don't feed you."

Ivar cranked up the heat in the truck, warmer than he normally had it, she guessed. She held her hands over a vent. "Is the forest here always that pretty?"

"Yes, but what do you mean specifically?"

She shrugged. "My lack of caffeine might be affecting my vision, but when we passed through that last clearing, the snow almost seemed suspended in midair. Like tiny crystals."

"Yeah, I noticed that too. I figured it was the light playing tricks. The sun and the snowmobile's headlight both reflecting off the snow."

"Probably." Unless the Yule vein was closer than she thought. All morning, branches had seemed to lift away as they approached, perfect clearings appearing when they needed to rest, the snow somehow less deep where they walked than it should have been. But she'd never heard of a Yule vein "doing magic."

Kringles used the energy of the lines to power the villages. That's all.

The Maple Mug Coffee House was cute and welcoming. Honey-colored floors gleamed softly beneath her boots, and garlands of pine and dried oranges hung between ceiling beams. Locals filled the tables, chatting over laptops and crossword puzzles.

And the aroma! She took a deep breath, filling her senses with espresso, baked cinnamon, maple syrup, and something nutty. It was heavenly, and as she exhaled, some of the tension in her shoulders eased.

Ivar caught her reaction and smiled. "See? Not so bad."

"It's homey. Like stepping into a Christmas card."

"That's Emma. She wants everyone to feel at home."

"Emma?"

"The owner." He nodded toward the counter, where a tall woman with dark hair and bright green eyes was laughing with a customer. "Now. What can I get you?"

"I can get it."

"My treat. I insist. Their butternut squash soup's the best in Vermont."

"Sounds wonderful. Oh, and a latte, please."

He ordered for both of them and joined her at a table near the woodstove.

"So," he said, placing two lattes and a table marker between them, "what exactly is your family business?"

Holly considered lying but decided honesty, or partial honesty, was simpler. "We manufacture toys."

For a heartbeat he stared, then burst out laughing. "No way."

"Way."

"You're serious?"

"I don't joke about toy production."

"Holly Kringle, toymaker." He shook his head, still smiling. "Next you'll say your dad's name is Chris."

"It's Adam. Chris is my grandfather."

Ivar laughed so hard she thought he might choke. When he finally caught his breath, he excused himself, then returned with two glasses of water, still grinning.

As he set the water down, they both reached for the same glass at the same time. Their fingers brushed, and they instinctively pulled back.

"Sorry," they said in perfect unison.

They stared at each other for a moment, then spoke again simultaneously: "You go ahead."

Holly couldn't help laughing. "Are we actually doing the speaking-in-sync thing?"

"Apparently." Ivar's eyes crinkled with amusement. "Jinx," he added, tapping the table.

"What are we, twelve?" But she was smiling despite herself.

"Buy me a coffee and I'll let you off the hook."

"I thought this was your treat."

"Smart and a toymaker. You're just full of surprises, Holly Kringle."

Before she could respond, the dark-haired woman approached

with two steaming bowls of soup and a plate of warm bread. "What's so funny over here, Ivar?"

"Emma, meet Holly Kringle. Holly's interested in the Hale property."

Emma smiled, setting the food down. "Nice to meet you. We were all sorry to see that land go up for sale. But Winterwood is a friendly place. Whatever you decide to do with it, you'll be welcome here."

"Thank you. That's very kind."

"Are you thinking resort? Vacation cabins?"

"Nothing like that. Right now we're just exploring."

"And what kind of business are you in?"

"Toys," Ivar said, and Holly braced for the reaction.

Emma blinked, then broke into a delighted laugh. "Of course you are. Well, in that case..." She pulled a flyer from her apron pocket and set it on the table. "Winterwood Christmas Carnival. It starts in a week. We have craft booths, carols, food, ice carving, you name it. We raise money so that every kid in town gets something special. On Christmas Eve, we have a breakfast with Santa event and hand out the gifts then. If your company wants to donate a few toys, we'd love that."

"I'll mention it to my father." Holly tucked the flyer into her bag.

"And if you're staying longer, we could always use another volunteer."

"I don't think I'll be here that long." At least she hoped not.

"Fair enough. Enjoy the soup. It will thaw your bones."

Holly tasted the soup and nearly melted. Silky, sweet, and rich with maple and nutmeg.

They ate in comfortable silence for a few minutes before Holly asked, "So where to next?"

Ivar leaned back in his chair. "You don't waste a minute."

"There's a lot to see."

"All work and no play."

She arched an eyebrow. "Is that a warning or an invitation?"

He grinned, eyes crinkling at the corners. "Maybe both. If you're serious about this land, you should see what it means to the people here. Not just the property lines. The heart of it."

"I don't really have time."

"Make time," he said, rising to his feet. "I have an idea."

She narrowed her eyes. "This is the part where I'm supposed to be suspicious, right?"

"Only if you hate fun."

The park ranger flashed her a grin that dared her to say no.

Whether it was that devilish smile or his blatant challenge, she didn't know, but she found herself caving. "Okay then." She stood, slipping the little maple-leaf cookie from her saucer into her pocket. "Lead the way."

YULE HAVE FUN, I PROMISE

<u>Ivar</u>

They passed the inn, stopping briefly so Ivar could collect Al from Liv's office. The husky bounded into the snow as if he'd been launched from a cannon, tail flying, nose buried in powder.

As they drove toward his cabin, Ivar's thoughts spun circles around one question: What on earth had he been thinking?

Bringing the polished, caffeine-fueled toy executive back to his home?

Maybe he'd lost his mind.

But deep down, he knew why he'd done it. He recognized that brittle energy in her voice, that need to control every variable. He'd lived that way until a few hard lessons stripped it out of him.

The truck crunched up his long, tree-lined drive. When the A-frame came into view, Holly leaned forward.

"Cute place."

"Thanks," he said, parking beside the porch. "It's my house."

Her eyebrows rose. "Seriously?"

"Seriously."

She gave the place a once-over, lips curving like she couldn't decide whether to laugh or groan. "Yeah. I totally see it."

They stepped out, and Al bounded ahead, circling the porch in wide, ecstatic loops.

"Stay inside where it's warm," Ivar said, opening the front door. "I need to grab a few things."

She nodded, glancing around. He watched her take in the fireplace, the books, the scuffed floorboards as if she were cataloguing details for a report. He wondered if she noticed that nothing in his cabin matched. The mugs were chipped, the rugs faded, the lamp held together with a bit of wire. Of course she did.

She touched the edge of his kitchen table, tracing a groove in the wood. "It's peaceful here." Soft, as though afraid to disturb the stillness.

He wanted to tell her that peace wasn't something you found. It was something you let in. But she was standing by the window, looking out at the pond dusted in snow, and he wondered, shutting the door and heading for the garage, if she was starting to understand.

He returned in ten minutes, his arms full of gear. "Come on."

She turned, startled, from her reverie. "We're going somewhere else?"

"Not far. To the pond."

As they stepped into the cold again, he handed her Liv's snow-suit. "Are we ice fishing? Because if this involves bait or sitting in the cold, I'm out."

He grinned. "We're not fishing."

"Then what are we doing?"

"Dog sledding. Al's been inside all day, and he needs to stretch his legs."

"Dog sledding?" She sounded incredulous. "With me?"

"Yup. Around the pond. It's Al's favorite thing."

"For some." She muttered. "And what kind of name is Al, anyway?"

"First name Al, last name Pine."

She blinked, then laughed. "Al Pine. That's terrible."

"That's what the shelter named him. We just call him Al."

"A humane society with a sense of humor."

"Exactly." He raised his voice. "Al! Dog sled!"

A crash echoed through the trees, and the husky appeared with fur dusted white and eyes gleaming with anticipation.

"See? Told you he loves it."

"Surely he's not strong enough to pull both of us."

"He's stronger than he looks. But we'll take turns."

Ivar hitched Al to the small sled and explained as he worked. "He knows the route. All you have to do is hang on."

He climbed on first, gave Al a pat, and called, "Hike!"

They shot forward, gliding across the edge of the frozen pond. The sled hissed over the snow, Al's harness jingling in rhythm. By the time they looped back, Holly's expression had shifted from skepticism to curiosity.

"See? Easy."

"I don't know about this." Her eyes narrowed. "Why do I think you're trying to scare me off the land?"

"I doubt you scare easily. Now, on you get. Sitting down."

She hesitated, but lowered herself onto the sled anyway. "The things I do for my family."

"Say 'Hike!' to go. 'Whoa!' to stop. Ready?"

Holly inhaled deeply. "Hike!"

Al surged forward, the sled jerking into motion. Ivar gave a quick push and watched as they circled the pond. There was Al and a flash of teal snowsuit, and a high-pitched yell.

At first it sounded like fear, but as she rounded the last corner, he heard genuine joy.

Holly was laughing.

"You're a natural," he called out.

When she returned, breathless and flushed, her eyes sparkled. "That was amazing. I think I'm addicted. Can I go again?"

"You sure can." Wow. He hadn't expected that.

He hadn't expected her.

She was an enigma. A contradiction wrapped in a teal snowsuit. And he wanted to know every layer of her story.

23
days until
Christmas Eve

MERRY LITTLE CRISIS

<u>Holly</u>

The smell of cinnamon drew Holly out of bed long before her alarm sounded.

She wasn't sure which was more intoxicating—the promise of coffee or the buttery sweetness wafting up the stairs. Either way, it beat the green smoothies she usually forced down before work.

Downstairs, a buffet of pastries sat under glass domes that could tempt the most disciplined of souls.

She poured herself a mug of coffee, still steaming, and claimed a cinnamon bun, then found a table by the window overlooking the forest. Snow clung to the pines, and the morning sun shimmered on the branches.

She opened her watch app, syncing her sleep data out of habit.

Eight full hours.

Her watch confirmed it: the best sleep she'd had in months.

Perhaps there was something to this whole "taking a break" thing after all. Not that she'd admit it to Rita.

Her phone pinged with a text. Rita. Was the woman clairvoyant?

Rita: I sent you the minutes from last night's meeting, as requested. But Holly, please. I know

you're there for work, but try to focus on a little relaxation, too. Include it on one of your to-do lists. And if you text me four times before 7 am again, I'm blocking you.
Holly: [saluting emoji]

She was scrolling through the meeting minutes, halfway through her bun, when she heard a long sigh behind her. Holly turned to see Liv at a nearby table, laptop open, brow furrowed.

With one more sigh, Liv closed the lid with a soft snap.

"I hope I didn't disturb you." Liv looked up apologetically. "But I'm getting so frustrated with this schedule. Organization isn't my strong suit, which I suppose isn't ideal for an innkeeper."

Holly smiled. "The inn seems perfectly organized to me."

"Oh, this place runs fine. It's the Winterwood Christmas Carnival that's got me tangled. So many moving pieces. Vendors, contests, volunteers. Last year's coordinator quit, and now it's all on me."

Carnival chaos. Holly could almost feel the spreadsheets forming in her brain. She didn't want to get involved, but the thought of leaving Liv stranded with a disorganized event made her twitch.

"May I join you?"

"Of course."

Holly grabbed her coffee and half-eaten bun and slid into the chair across from her. "I might be able to help. Organizing is sort of my thing. Ask my assistant. I'm known as the queen of spreadsheets."

Liv looked hopeful. "Really? You're sure? I wouldn't want to take you away from your project."

"Nonsense. This will be a nice break." She grinned. "Besides, after yesterday, I think I've earned an indoor activity."

"Yesterday?" Liv poured Holly another coffee.

Holly hesitated, then laughed. "Your brother took me dog sledding."

Liv's eyebrows shot up. "He did? I'm impressed. Ivar doesn't let just anyone take the sled. How'd you manage?"

"My family... where I live... I'm used to sleigh rides, but nothing like that. So I screamed." Holly said honestly, then corrected herself with a small smile. "But mostly laughed. I haven't done that in a while, and I think I kind of needed it."

Liv's expression softened. "That sounds exactly like him. He pretends he's not a softie, but he's all heart. I'm just glad he didn't scare you off. Now, let me show you this mess I call a festival plan."

She opened her laptop again, turning it so Holly could see. The document was a maze of notes, ice delivery times, vendor contracts, event schedules, and more. It was chaos.

"Okay." Holly scanned through it. "Give me an hour and I'll give you a checklist that'll run smoother than Santa's toy route."

Liv blinked. "Are you serious?"

"I am. Trust me. I do this for a living."

Liv shook her head in disbelief. "All right, I'll bring you more coffee and get out of your way."

An hour and four coffees later, Holly closed the laptop with a satisfied sigh. She'd built a color-coded schedule, linked the contact list to each event file, and created reminders for every major deadline.

She found Liv at the reception desk. "Here you go." Holly handed the laptop over. "Everything's updated. You'll have this festival running like clockwork."

Liv glanced at the screen, her eyes widening. "Holly, this is incredible." She set the laptop down and, before Holly could protest, wrapped her in a spontaneous hug. "You saved me!"

Holly froze, startled. Hugs weren't standard protocol at the North-east Division, at least not in her office. But a warmth rose in her chest all the same.

"You're welcome." The smile came easily—unexpected, but not un-welcome.

Just then, a gust of cold air swept through the lobby as the front door opened. Ivar stepped inside, brushing snow off his jacket.

"Well, speak of the ranger." Liv turned. "Guess who saved the Winterwood Christmas Carnival? Holly! I was drowning in chaos, and she swooped in with spread-sheets and checklists and... poof! Order restored."

Ivar raised an eyebrow. "Spread-sheet Holly performed a little magic?"

Holly laughed. "Not magic. Experience. Though the line's been known to blur."

"Careful." Ivar's mouth quirked at the corner. "Around here, being good at something can get you volunteered for a lot more work."

Liv winked. "Don't tempt me."

Holly took another sip of coffee, hiding her grin. The banter between Liv and Ivar reminded her of her own siblings before they were scattered across the globe. Memories of teasing and laughter, a time when life was simpler. Memories that filled her with warmth.

STOCKING UP ON EXCUSES

<u>Holly</u>

"About yesterday," Ivar said as the truck climbed deeper into the forest, "I hope I didn't make you uncomfortable with the dog sledding. You were a good sport about it, but I crossed a line."

"You didn't. Honest. It was unexpected, but also fun." Holly watched sunlight flicker through bare branches. "I'm a big girl. If I didn't want to do it, I'd have said no."

"Yeah, but still..." His hands tightened on the steering wheel. "The thing is, I know what it's like to bury yourself in work until it stops being healthy."

That caught her off guard. "I thought you loved your job."

"I do. But before this, I did something else."

She turned, studying him. "What? Lumberjack? Official maple syrup tester?"

"Video game developer."

She blinked. "You're joking."

"No, ma'am." His mouth curved, but not quite into a smile. "Ten years."

She tried to picture this plaid-shirted outdoorsman behind a desk, under artificial light, typing code instead of trudging through snow. "I know we just met, but I can't picture it."

"Yeah. Most people can't."

"So, what happened?"

"That," he said, turning off onto a narrow side road, "is a story for another time. Because we're here."

The truck slowed, tires crunching to a stop at the trailhead.

Ivar reached behind the seat and handed her a pair of snowshoes. "You'll want these."

They got out, boots sinking into the powder. Today, she'd left her tablet behind, opting instead for her laminated, color-coded map courtesy of her father. She laid it across the truck's hood to get her bearings. Ivar leaned closer, the faint scent of cedar and wood smoke following him. It was quite pleasant.

"I can't get over this map. Do you have friends at NASA?"

"Not quite." She hid a smile.

He pointed to a ridge on the east side of the forest. "We're here. We'll cut across to the basin. That's where I've had the strongest feeling."

"Feeling?"

"Never mind. It's nothing."

Placing a hand on his arm, she said, "I'd really like it if you told me."

He rubbed the back of his neck, then reached into his coat pocket. "I have no idea why I'm showing you this, but... here."

His map looked like it had survived a blizzard and then a decade in a drawer. The paper was worn thin, creased into soft squares. Hand-drawn grids, penciled notes, and dates overlapped like ghosts of past searches.

"No wonder you like mine. Yours looks like it was printed during the Reagan administration."

"What can I say? It's well-used. I started marking it up about three years ago. I've been searching for the place I wandered to while lost when I was a kid."

Her eyebrows lifted. "Lost, as in rescue-mission lost?"

"Yeah. I was eight and somehow wandered away from my family. I ended up staying out in the forest overnight. And it was in the winter."

He traced a finger around one rough circle on the map.

"I found shelter under a tree." Ivar's voice went quiet. "I don't remember all of it, but I was warm. And I wasn't afraid. Not really. Most likely, I was in shock. Or maybe…"

His voice trailed off. "I guess I got lucky."

"A tree kept you warm?" She forced her tone light, but her pulse had begun to race. Surprisingly, her watch didn't start beeping, because this was exciting. This might be a clue as to the location of the Yule vein. "Not just sheltered from the snow. You're sure?"

He didn't look at her, obviously uncomfortable. But he continued all the same.

"Yeah. It sounds ridiculous, but there was something about it. Even as a child, I knew it wasn't like the other trees. You're going to think I'm crazy, and I'm not sure why I'm telling you this, but it's like it had an aura. It didn't glow, but..." He shrugged. "Kind of vibrated with energy. That memory haunts me to this day, so I've been searching for it to find the truth. I don't think I want to be right. I'm kind of hoping that it's simply a species not typically found in this area."

For a moment, neither of them spoke. The forest seemed to still around them. And in that silence, the whisper of a memory she hadn't touched in years surfaced.

Growing up, all the kids heard the legend of the Yule Tree. It was the epicenter of Christmas power. The place where every magical line began.

No one knew where it came from, or how old it was, but its roots extended across the globe as energy veins, providing the magical power that generated the Santa workshops. Wherever it was, the surrounding land thrived. The air itself grew softer. And those lucky enough to stand beneath its boughs would feel it. A warmth that went beyond skin and bone, as if the forest itself had welcomed them.

The story was older than Santa. Most believed it to be nothing more than a myth about the origins of the magical Yule veins. But now, hearing Ivar's quiet, matter-of-fact words, Holly wondered if the myth was reality in the Winterwood forest.

She folded her map, forcing her voice steady. "Well, I hope we both find what we came for."

"You're mocking me, aren't you?"

"No. I told you my search here was about vibes. How different is that from what you're after?"

He stared at her for the longest time. "Fine. Let's get going."

They snowshoed through the woods for a couple of hours, following deer trails and unmarked ridges. Ivar led the way, pausing now and then to jot a note or take a picture. Holly kept pace (despite the burning in her legs), pretending to focus on the topography when really her thoughts looped around his story.

The legend of the Yule Tree made for schoolyard stories and songs. Trees that glowed. Forests that whispered your name. People didn't take them seriously. Not her family. Not her.

But hearing it from someone like Ivar—grounded, logical, so unmistakably human—made her wonder if there was some truth to it all.

And if she found such a tree, what it would do for her career.

By the time they returned to the truck, the sun was lowering into the trees, turning the snow pale rose and blue. Holly's legs ached to the point where bending over to unbuckle her snowshoes was almost impossible.

The second time she winced, Ivar came to her rescue. "Sore legs?" he asked.

"You have no idea." Her attempt to suppress an embarrassed laugh failed. "I think if you weren't here, I'd be in these for days."

"Don't worry," he replied with a chuckle. "It's more common that you think."

"It is?"

"No. Not at all."

Holly laughed outright, nearly losing her balance in the process. "Glad to know I'm setting new records in athletic grace."

He bent to help, still grinning. "You're doing great for someone who may never walk again."

Their hands brushed as he bent over. It was brief, perhaps half a second, but it was enough to send an unexpected spark through her and chase off the winter chill. She brushed at her coat as if that would wipe the feeling away, grateful Ivar's attention was on her feet.

As soon as he'd eased her feet out of the snowshoes, she turned to toss her pack in the cab.

And froze.

Nestled against a bag in Ivar's truck bed was her broom.

Her. Broom.

For a moment she could only stare. It was as still as a regular old broom, yet a faint, electric pull made her bones practically buzz. How long had it been there? She hadn't touched it since the night she arrived.

Had it come to her in the forest? To Ivar's truck? That was crazier than Ivar's magical tree.

His voice broke through her daze. "When did you toss that in there?"

"Right before we left. I told you it's a good luck charm."

He raised a brow. "I thought you said it was for sweeping away bad first impressions."

"That too. It's kind of a family thing." She managed a faint smile.

"Okay." He nodded, apparently satisfied, and turned back to the cab.

"You know, you surprise me more and more each day."

Holly climbed in and stared straight ahead as the truck rumbled to life.

Outside, the forest blurred by. Inside, her thoughts refused to still.

She was supposed to be here to assess logistics. Not legends. Scout a site, go home.

But Ivar Nilsen was searching for a tree that matched the description of a legend. And now, her broom wanted to join the search.

Something was happening in Winterwood. But what?

OH WHAT FUN IT IS TO SPY

<u>Ivar</u>

The stillness of the ranger station was almost suspicious.

Ivar leaned back in his chair, boots crossed at the ankle, one hand loosely holding a lukewarm tea. Across the room, Al lay in his usual spot under the desk, snoring softly with legs twitching like he was chasing snow hares in his dreams.

After dropping off Holly, Ivar had stopped by work to finish a few reports, despite it being his week off.

But his mind was somewhere else entirely.

Scratch that. His mind was entirely filled with her. With Holly. And with the odd swirl of things that seemed to follow them since her arrival: talk of vibes, special trees, and weird old brooms.

None of it should have made sense. Yet somehow, it did. She did.

Strangest of all, he trusted her. Instinctively. Otherwise, why would he have told her about the tree? That story had never left his lips before. That kind of comfort wasn't like him. Usually, it took months for him to lower his guard. And he'd known her for less than seventy-two hours.

He didn't know what was weirder—the way she hadn't balked when he mentioned a tree with an aura or that she had him acting so unlike himself.

The cursor blinked on a half-written wildlife survey. With a sigh, Ivar rubbed a hand over his face and opened a new tab.

His fingers hovered above the keys. Research, he told himself. Nothing more than a background check of the potential land buyer. That's all.

He typed: Holly Kringle.

And hit Enter.

Because of her name, a wide but unsurprising list of results came up. Holiday websites, craft blogs, corporate Christmas marketing. But nothing on her. So, he refocused the search: Holly Kringle toy manufacturer, Kringle family corporation, Adam Kringle toy expansion and so forth.

How could there be no mention of Holly or her family company? She was definitely the type to work on multiple charity boards and post articles on LinkedIn about corporate policy and women executives.

He was close to giving up when he found a rabbit hole: obscure forums, fringe subreddits, conspiracy pages in dated fonts.

"Is Santa real?"

"The Great Kringle Cover-Up."

"Confirmed: Toy production facilities in Northern Quebec disguised as weather stations."

He scoffed, but clicked anyway.

Stories unfolded about people who claimed to have seen "Kringle operatives" at airports, loading suspicious wooden crates onto small planes. One post told of a reporter who had "proof" that Santa existed but mysteriously published a puff piece about Alaskan artisans instead.

Another claimed that Santa Claus didn't use elves but had a magical village for their human workers. Some said there was one Santa. Others claimed there was a network of interconnected Santas.

Halfway through a comment thread about chimney teleportation, a loud THWACK made him jump.

The door of the station had slammed shut. Carla, one of the part-time trail coordinators, breezed in holding a clipboard.

"Hey, Ivar. Aren't you on vacation?" She dropped the clipboard on his desk as he slammed his laptop closed.

"I came by to catch up on a few things."

"Oh yeah? Working hard or hardly working?" she teased, peering at him suspiciously. "Why do you look guilty?"

"You caught me. I'm trying to figure out what to get Lloyd for Christmas. I drew his name for the Secret Santa exchange."

Al let out a sleepy woof under the desk, stretching his paws toward Ivar's foot.

Carla thought for a moment. "Get him a Yeti travel mug. I'm tired of him spilling coffee all over the truck. Goodness knows why he uses a regular mug. I had to redo a report last week thanks to his coffee stains."

"Good idea."

"Anytime, chief. Now go home." Carla shook her head as she turned to leave. "You two need a hobby."

As soon as the door shut, the lap-top opened again. "I think I have one now."

Holly

Holly paced the worn rug in sock feet, robe belted tight over plaid pajamas. The map lay open on the desk, but she wasn't looking at it. Not yet.

Her eyes flicked to the corner. To the broom.

"I know you're trying to tell me something." The words came out as a mutter. "You followed me to Winterwood. You turned up in the forest. I get it. I'm listening."

The broom leaned in silence, its straw bristles curled with age. Rough-hewn and handmade, craft-ed in Italy ages ago and carved from the Tree of the Ancients. La Befana's voice echoed in her mind. "When the time comes, it will guide you to the truth your heart has forgotten."

Holly's legs went weak, so she sat at the small desk. At the time, she'd chalked those words up to poetic ceremony. The broom was a tool. Transportation. Like a sleigh. Like a snowmobile. Like any other piece of operational equipment.

But what if it was more than that? It had followed her to Winterwood of its own free will, and now, she was talking to it. She didn't talk to her car. Or her sleigh. Neither of those followed her around. So... what did that mean?

Growing up around magic meant never questioning its existence. But she'd always seen it as infra-structure. An energy grid to be harnessed, measured, forecasted, and distributed. Magic as logistics.

And yet, Ivar had said a tree had helped him. Not covered him. Not sheltered him. Helped. It had kept him warm through the night.

Her fingers twitched.

That wasn't systemized magic. That was… intent.

Ivar's tree. The Yule Tree. The Tree of the Ancients.

With a slow exhale, her focus returned to the map. She smoothed the crinkled edge, appreciating the topographical lines, color-coded markers, GPS overlays, and coordinates. Comfort. Structure. Logic.

Then she pulled out Ivar's map.

It was everything hers wasn't—hand-drawn grids, smudged pencil notes, a faint coffee stain in the corner, some tree doodles along the edges. Messy. Real. Totally him.

She should've laughed it off.

Instead, she placed them side by side under the lamplight.

The crossed-out sections and directional arrows all seemed to orbit a patch of forest that didn't even appear on hers. A blank spot. A gap. A pocket of nothing.

Her finger tapped at that spot, and her eyes returned to the broom.

"Is this it? Is this where we're supposed to go?"

The broom didn't move. Or did it? No. The floor creaked. Old houses did that, right?

A sigh escaped as she rubbed her forehead. "I'm not doing this. I'm not becoming that Kringle. The one who talks to brooms and follows breadcrumbs into the woods like she's in a Christmas movie."

The broom said nothing.

"I'm a businesswoman. I run supply chains. Forecast global toy logistics. I don't believe in—"

A whoosh of air brushed past her, making the curtains stir, but the window was closed.

Then the fire flared, just for a heartbeat. Shadows stretched along the far wall like reaching branches, then melted back.

Holly's breath caught.

Another look at the broom, voice barely above a whisper. "You really are trying to tell me something, aren't you?"

The air in the room held still but charged, as if full of static waiting to spark.

Her finger slid across the map, stopping over the blank spot that pulsed in her mind like a heartbeat.

Because she knew where that blank spot might lead them.

To the Yule Tree.

A legend no more.

And if her broomstick had been carved from that same ancient lineage, then of course it would be drawn there. But how had it known when she left home, and why now?

Her head throbbed with more questions than answers. Resting her head in her hands, she stared at the spot on Ivar's map until she reached the only conclusion there was. "I'll go." The words came softly as her gaze slid to the broom. "We'll go. But if you pull any magic-stunt nonsense in front of Ivar, I will donate you to the nearest charity shop."

The curtains settled. The fire crackled.

And Holly climbed into bed, her mind racing.

Decisions were familiar territory. But this was different. Uncovering a legend might have consequences she couldn't begin to predict. And of course, it might not be anything, but if it was the Yule Tree... then what?

It was far too soon to share her suspicions with her father. Calling him up and causing a stir over unfounded suspicions might derail any chance at promotion. But presenting proof? That was a game changer.

Ivar would need the coordinates so he could plan for tomorrow. But it was after nine, and texting him at this hour felt oddly intimate, given they'd never texted before.

How to begin? "Hey, Ivar, it's me." No, because what if she came up as an unknown number? And "hey" was far too familiar. "Hello" sounded weirdly formal. She decided on, "It's Holly Kringle. I have a suggestion for tomorrow." Unfortunately, that's not what she typed.

Holly: It's Kringle.

Trying to backspace and fix her mistake, she hit enter and grimaced when three dots appeared.

Ivar: Copy that, Kringle. Ranger here. Over.

She laughed, despite her embarrassment.

Holly: I have a suggestion for where to start tomorrow.
Ivar: Copy that. Please send mission coordinates.

Laughing harder now, she sent him the location.

Ivar: Document received. Mission commences at 0900. Goodnight, Kringle.
(pause)
Holly: Goodnight, Ranger.

Holly set her phone to charge and turned out the light. Closing her eyes, she willed her thoughts to still. But instead of spreadsheets and site plans or even thoughts of the Yule Tree , she saw a quiet pond, a cozy cabin, and a certain park ranger's smile.

He believed in a magical tree. If she revealed herself, would he believe in her?

22
days until
Christmas Eve

SLEIGH WHAT?

Holly

Coffee. She needed coffee.

Sleep had abandoned her around three, leaving her tossing and turning, wondering if she should tell someone her suspicions. Rita? Her father? Her brother Henry? This was his kind of thing.

But she'd done nothing. Evidence first. Then the frenzy at HQ.

She entered the lobby on sore, stiff legs, and poured a coffee, unable to wait until she found a table in the dining room.

"How's the coffee?" Liv called from behind the counter. Her hair was in a festive braid, a candy-cane striped apron tied snug over a red sweater that read Yule Be Sorry.

"Wonderful and exactly what I need." Holly took another sip. "So, do you always dress like a walking Christmas pun?"

"Only from November 1st to December 26th. I have plenty more where this came from if you'd like to borrow something."

Holly laughed. "I'm good. Thanks. But I bet my assistant would pay good money to see me in one of those."

Liv poured herself a coffee, then gestured to the clipboard on the counter. "Before you sit, quick question. Do you happen to know how to run a raffle booth?"

Holly blinked. "Oddly enough, that's not on my resume."

"Oh well then, the search continues. Speaking of searches, how is yours going?"

"Fine. Good, I suppose."

"And Ivar?"

"He's a good tour guide."

"He does love that forest. I love him dearly, but he can get a bit obsessed with it. Always has done. That's why I was so surprised he moved to California. But..." A shrug. "Then he came back."

"He told me. That's why he took me dog sledding. Apparently, I reminded him of himself. A workaholic who needed to have fun." Was there something in the coffee here that made her open up, or was it Liv's charm? A Nilsen family trait, apparently.

"Don't let him fool you. He still works all the time, but being here close to his forest and surrounded by friends, there's a bit more of a balance. Now let's get you some breakfast before you head back out. It's a cold one today."

Holly was finishing her breakfast when her phone buzzed.

Ivar: On time for 0900.

"What's got you all smiling this morning?" Liv asked, refreshing Holly's coffee cup.

"Sorry, what?" Holly asked.

"Oh, just commenting on how happy you look."

"I do?"

"You do. And I'm guessing that text wasn't about work."

"Of course it was work-related." It came out a bit too fast, and she caught Liv's knowing smile.

"If you say so."

BROOM FOR TWO

<u>Holly</u>

As Ivar packed the lunch Liv had made into his pack, Holly slid her broomstick—deliberately this time—into the side loops of her backpack. Ivar's eyes snagged on it. He tilted his head as if he wanted to ask but thought better of it.

"Family tradition, right?" he said instead.

"Something like that." Casual. She hoped she sounded casual.

He nodded once, as if filing it away. Then he handed her a thermos and gestured toward her map. "So the location you sent me is in a secluded valley. It's pretty remote and not exactly ideal for toy distribution and manufacturing. Why would that spot even interest you?"

Deflection seemed like her best option, so she handed him his map, the one she'd borrowed. "Thanks for letting me use this. Comparing the two helped me narrow things down."

"Okay. A—you're avoiding my question. And B—I don't see how my map could help you make a business decision." The map slid carefully into his coat pocket. "You're a bit of a mystery, and since I'm curious by nature, I did a little research last night."

"You Googled me?" There was no need to panic. Sure, there were a few truths about her family online, but they were buried under so many falsehoods it was unlikely he'd figured anything out.

Last night, she'd wondered what would happen if he learned the truth. But that didn't mean she'd actually tell him. Still... would it really be so bad if he had?

"I did. And I couldn't find a thing about you or your family. No business filings, no press mentions. Nothing." At least he had the decency to look sheepish.

"Well, good. Because I'm a very private person. My family is too."

"There was no shortage of hits on the Kringle name though."

Holly laughed, hoping it sounded natural and not stressed. "Of course. That should hardly be surprising. Or were you expecting to find me blogging about Christmas decorations?"

"Believe me, that did not cross my mind at all."

Wow, that stung in a weird kind of way. Of course she'd never blog about Christmas decorations, but she was a Santa. Didn't she give off some kind of Christmas presence?

"I didn't realize how many Santa theories there are."

"Ah. So you toured online forums and conspiracy threads."

"Well, the internet does love a good conspiracy theory," he said, flashing her a rueful smile.

"Oh, Ivar." She gave him a playful bump. Never in her life had she imagined wanting to reveal her secret to someone—especially to someone she'd known for mere days. Days! But she did. She really, truly did.

He'd think she was crazy.

Or would he?

The risk wasn't worth it. Not if this turned out to be a wild-goose chase and there was no Yule Tree.

And yet... the thought lingered. A crush? Fresh air? The altitude? Or maybe his smile. Whatever it was, the urge to tell him everything was getting harder to resist.

They drove as far as they could before setting off on snow-shoes. The sun filtered in patches through the trees, and the deeper they went, the quieter everything became.

At first, it was the ordinary hush of snow. Then, even that began to change. The wind stilled. No branches cracked. No birds called. The forest felt almost watchful.

"Is it always this quiet out here?" Holly asked.

"Not usually." Ivar slowed, scanning the canopy.

Holly followed his gaze and watched as a few ravens circled high above, their black wings catching stray beams of light that seemed to shift in a kaleidoscope of directions.

When she looked down, the snow underfoot wasn't smooth anymore. It gathered in faint, curling patterns, like ripples leading forward, forming a trail. There was no denying it now: magic stirred in the forest, its signs growing stronger with every step.

"Do you see that?" she asked.

"The snow?"

"Those lines. They almost look like arrows."

Ivar crouched, brushing gloved fingers along the pattern. "We must be on an animal trail, and the wind is blowing the loose snow." But he didn't sound convinced. Checking his compass, he said, "We're still headed the right way."

A few paces later, a pair of deer stood watching them from the trees, their dark eyes unblinking. A squirrel clung to a trunk nearby, still as a statue.

"Is it just me, or does it seem like those animals are waiting for us to pass?" Ivar asked, his voice low.

"It's not just you."

"Animals act differently before a storm. But no storms were forecast for today."

She'd only taken a few more steps when the humming began—a low thrum that vibrated through the earth.

Was this what her father had meant for her to feel? The living pulse of a Yule vein? She'd lived above one all her life and had never noticed this sensation. Had she simply stopped detecting it, the way you stop hearing the steady rhythm of a fan? Or was this something new? Something... waiting?

Because now, with each step, it grew stronger. It wasn't just beneath her feet. It was inside her, in her bones and breath, a steady deep rhythm that urged her forward. Not like a hand tugging, but like gravity remembering her name.

Never had anything reached for her like this. Called to her.

Chosen her.

The weight of her broom grew heavy against her shoulder, and she slowed to adjust the strap. She wasn't afraid, but falling into step beside Ivar instead of ahead was a comfort. His nearness steadied her, the pull of him almost as irresistible as the one pulling her forward.

She glanced up. Light filtered through the branches, catching his face in fractured glints that made him seem almost otherworldly. Forest and man blending until she couldn't tell where one ended, and the other began.

She blinked away the image.

"Keep going," he said. "We're close." And in that moment, she knew it was calling to him too.

Her fingers brushed the broom handle at her side to find it vibrating.

They continued, the wind blowing away the snow to form a path.

"This is off every trail I've ever taken. We're heading toward the canyon edge. I'm not sure how we're going to get down there."

Not if. But how. Because they both knew instinctively that they must.

A strong, sudden gust of wind whipped through the trees, causing the broom to pulse harder against her side. Then it lurched forward in a burst, sending her face-first into the snow.

"What happened?" Ivar crouched beside her, offering his hand.

"It's the tree. Your tree. I know you hear it calling you."

He opened his mouth, then closed it again. His eyes darted toward the horizon. "I..." he began, but before he could say more, the broom shot forward again, this time knocking Holly into him, and they both tumbled into the snow.

"What the heck is going on?" Ivar snapped. "I need answers, Holly. Now."

"The tree, Ivar. It's calling us. You know it is." She tossed her gloves aside, her fingers shaking as she unstrapped the broom, holding it tightly. "We need to go."

It trembled once. Then again, like a bird ready to take flight. She turned back to Ivar, his expression a mix of fear, disbelief, and wonder. The broom tugged again. She swung a leg over it and held out her hand. "Leave your bag with mine and climb on."

He didn't move. "Holly—"

"Please, Ivar." She met his eyes and held him there. Pleading.

"I don't understand."

"I know. But I need you to trust me."

He hesitated for one heartbeat, maybe two, before dropping his bag and climbing on. "You sure about this?"

"Not at all," she said, smiling faintly. "Now hold on tight. It's been a while since I've done this."

"Wait. What?" he said, his question turning into a yell as they lifted.

The trees fell away beneath them. Wind rushed past. Snowflakes sparkled like stars. The forest became a patchwork of white and green, and Holly laughed from the rush of it all. How she'd missed this.

And Ivar? He groaned behind her, his grip on her waist tightening as they soared forward, then suddenly down, descending into a clearing of untouched snow.

TREE'S COMPANY

<u>Ivar</u>

The moment his boots hit the snow, Ivar bent double and retched into a nearby snowbank. His head spun. He'd flown. On a broomstick. In the sky. How could any of this be real?

Maybe he'd hit his head last week helping Eli hang Christmas lights, and he'd been in a coma ever since. Either that or his research into the Kringle family had been a waste of time because Holly Kringle—beautiful, infuriating, impossible Holly—wasn't related to Santa Claus.

She was a witch.

He turned to find her, half afraid she'd turn him into a frog, and froze.

The clearing stretched out around them, hushed and perfect, with snow lying thick on the ground. But it was the tree at the center that held him.

It towered over every tree in the area and was alive in a way that defied everything he knew about life. Its bark shimmered faintly, like moonlight breathing through wood grain. Light threaded through the branches, not from any visible source but from within—silver and gold, shifting like embers. The air itself pulsed to an invisible rhythm, as though the forest had a heartbeat.

"This is it," he whispered. "This is the tree."

He took a step closer. An ache rose behind his ribs that was half wonder, half recognition. As a boy, he'd stumbled into the woods terrified and lost, and the light had found him, protected him, and wrapped him in warmth.

The truth hit him with force. He hadn't imagined it. And now, the tree welcomed him back, as if it had been waiting.

Holly stood several yards away, utterly still. Her expression was somewhere between awe and surrender. For a long moment, he didn't move, afraid to disturb her communion. Then he saw the glint of a tear sliding down her cheek.

He crossed the snow quietly, removed his gloves, and slipped his hand into hers.

The moment their fingers touched, the air around them stirred. A faint hum rose. It was low, melodic, and not sound so much as vibration. The wind lifted, swirling the snow into slow spirals around the clearing. The snow at their feet began to glow with a soft, pulsing light that spread outward in concentric circles.

Holly gasped, her fingers tightening around his. "Do you feel that?"

"Yes," he answered, though he wasn't sure either of them had spoken aloud.

Warmth spread from their joined hands, up his arm, through his chest. Her heartbeat synced with his own, matching the pulse of the earth.

The branches above them swayed despite the absence of wind, and the roots of the tree became visible beneath the snow—a glowing lattice spreading outward, and up, up, through the earth and into them both, pulsing with the same silvery light that ran through the trunk.

Then, as suddenly as it began, the phenomenon subsided, leaving only a subtle shimmer that seemed to emanate from the tree's very essence.

They stood hand in hand in the hush that followed, breathing in unison.

"You didn't imagine it," she whispered.

"No," he said, voice rough with wonder. "I suppose not."

"I thought... we all thought it was a myth."

"We?" he asked. "Like other witches?"

That earned a laugh, and she turned to him. "No. Not like other witches. I'll tell you everything, but not here. Not now. For the moment, let's just be... here."

He looked from the tree to her, and the shimmer of light seemed to live within her, threading through her skin like starlight made flesh. In that moment, the forest faded, and she was all he saw. Radiant. Impossible. She was the most beautiful thing he'd ever known.

For a heartbeat, everything—her, the forest, the light—was bound together, bound to him. His entire world. Everything he needed. All that he wanted.

The snow swirled once more, then drifted down in silence. The image softened but didn't fade; it lingered—quiet, steady, and achingly real.

When he finally found his voice again, it came out as barely more than a whisper. "What does this mean?"

Her eyes shone, reflecting the gold around them. "I was hoping you could tell me. You were the one meant to find it."

He swallowed hard, the truth of it settling deep. "We were."

The tree from his childhood wasn't a dream. It was real, and it had chosen now to reveal itself.

He didn't understand why, and maybe he didn't need to. All that mattered was Holly's hand in his and the certainty in his heart that he was exactly where he was meant to be.

Holly leaned her head against his shoulder. He squeezed her hand gently, getting a squeeze back, the echo of the warmth still thrumming beneath their palms.

Neither of them spoke. Neither of them had to. Something had changed, as profound as the roots beneath their feet and as vast as the sky above. He didn't yet know what it was, but he welcomed it with open arms.

BREWED AWAKENINGS

<u>Holly</u>

They sat near the back of the Maple Mug, close together in the corner booth, two conspirators hiding from the world. Neither had spoken much. The forest had felt too sacred to disturb, and by the time they had reached the truck via broom travel, Ivar had doubled over again, hands on his knees, breathing hard before losing his lunch into the snow.

Now, inside the cafe, he remained pale but steadier.

"Again, I'm sorry about the motion sickness," Holly said quietly.

"I guess you get used to it," he managed, attempting a smile that didn't quite reach his eyes. The tremor beneath his words wasn't only from nausea.

Emma arrived with their lattes, cheerful as ever. "Here you go. You two look like you could use some warming up. Sure you don't want a seat by the fire?"

"We're fine, thank you," Holly replied, forcing a polite smile. She would have preferred privacy—her room at the inn, his cabin—but Ivar had insisted on somewhere normal, surrounded by chatter and clinking cups. She understood. He needed reality to anchor him.

Emma glanced between them. "Are you okay, Ivar?"

"Fine," he said quickly. "Just something I ate."

"I hope not from here."

"No, of course not. Some questionable leftovers."

Emma didn't seem convinced, but she moved away all the same.

Holly took a sip of her latte to steady herself. What had happened between them today had shaken her, though not as much as it had shaken poor Ivar, and she wanted to reassure him.

"It's true, isn't it?" Ivar said finally, voice low. "The things I read about your family."

"I'm not sure what you read," she said, keeping her voice gentle, "but I'll tell you the truth. About me. About my family." Hours before, she'd only wanted to tell him. And now, here they were. She didn't need to ask him to guard her secret. He already understood. Somehow, she knew he always would.

Reaching across the table before she could second-guess herself , she wrapped her fingers around his. The moment their hands met, the faint echo of the Yule Tree pulsed beneath their skin. Ivar's eyes flicked up to hers, startled, but he didn't pull away.

"Everything I've told you is true-ish. My name is Holly Kringle, and yes, my family manufactures toys for Christmas." She took a deep breath. "We also deliver them on Christmas Eve because we're Santas."

He blinked. "Santas? Plural?"

"The world's too big for one Santa, so my family spreads the work around. My father and aunt oversee the global operation; the rest of us manage regions. I'm the Santa of the Northeast."

She paused, watching him absorb the words.

After a long sip of latte, he said, "Maybe we should've gone somewhere I could get something stronger."

"I wouldn't blame you." His hand had trembled slightly when he lifted the cup, so she tightened her grip on the one she still held as her way of saying, I'm here.

He replied with a small nod. "I'll be okay. Please continue."

"Um, well, we live in hidden villages all over the world. We employ regular people, not elves. Some stay for generations; others leave for the outside world. It's a choice. And on Christmas Eve, the Santas deliver the toys."

"How?"

"Santa magic."

He raised a brow. "You say that like it's scientific fact."

"It is. But it's fairly limited stuff. Here's the Cliff Notes version: we can make sleighs fly, deliver toys, decorate rooms, craft magical toys, disguise ourselves as the iconic Santa, and pull off a few small tricks." She nodded at his latte. "Case in point."

He glanced down. The leaf Emma had drawn in the foam had reshaped itself into a perfect Santa face.

He stared. "How—"

"Santa magic."

He leaned back, exhaling. "So your entire family are Santas?"

"Yes and no. All Santas are Kringles, but not all Kringles are Santas. My brother Henry and my cousin Jack have a different sort of magic. I'm assuming you've heard of Jack Frost."

He held up a hand. "Okay. Stop there. My brain's already at capacity. Just tell me about the tree. What does it mean? Why were you looking for it?"

"I wasn't, not exactly," she said, tracing a circle on the table's surface. "I was looking for the power it gives off. There are veins of magical power under the earth. We call them Yule veins. They sustain our towns, our work. But the Yule Tree? It was thought to be an ancient legend. And according to this legend, all Yule veins stem from that one tree. Its roots reach across the world."

Ivar rubbed his temples. "So finding it means... what? Unlimited power?"

"I have no idea. As far as I'm aware, no one has ever seen a Yule Tree. I should be home right now, telling my father. But it hasn't sunk in. I feel—" She searched for the word. "—humbled. Small."

"Yeah," he said softly, his eyes on her, studying her, and seeing her in a way that left her unguarded. She shifted in her seat, not to hide from him, but from the surprise of wanting to open herself to him.

Finally, he asked, "And me? How do I fit into all this?"

Her eyes lifted to his. "I have no idea, but it must be because you found the Yule Tree as a child."

He nodded slowly, then looked down at their still-joined hands.

"So when we touched back there, we..."

"Connected," Holly finished. "Like we were part of each other and..."

"Part of the forest."

A gentle silence settled between them. The noise of the cafe fell away, replaced by the soft beat of their connected pulse. They'd shared something rare and beautiful; they were connected, bound by something she couldn't name.

After a moment, he cleared his throat, his voice rough. "One more question before my head explodes."

She smiled. "Go ahead."

"What's up with the broom?"

His question brought them back to reality, back to the coffee house. "That," she laughed, "will cost you another latte."

BRANCHING OUT

<u>Ivar</u>

It took every ounce of strength Ivar had to sit and listen as Holly spoke about magic, and Santas, and power veins beneath the earth.

Now she was describing an Italian tradition—La Befana, a woman who rode a broom delivering gifts to children, how she was a distant branch of the Kringle family tree, and how that broom was carved from the tree they'd come across today. Holly said it all so matter-of-factly, as if ancient magic and airborne grandmothers were as normal as gravity.

But it wasn't normal. None of it was. His entire definition of reality had shifted somewhere between the moment he threw his leg over a broomstick and the moment he realized the tree was humming, breathing, and living beneath his skin.

And yet... while standing before that tree, hand in hand with Holly, nothing had ever felt more right.

"I think it's time I dropped you back at the inn," he said at last, his voice quieter than he intended. "I need to go lie down."

"Of course," she said. "And I should let my family know. But I'll walk from here. It's not far. I just need the stuff out of your truck."

He wanted to protest, to drive her to the inn, but exhaustion pressed down on him like snowfall. "Okay," he murmured.

By the time he reached his cabin, the world had narrowed to muscle memory: boots off, jacket half-hung on a chair, lights left on. He barely made it to the couch before sleep claimed him.

And then he was back in the forest.

The clearing stretched wide and still, moonlight glinting off the snow. The Yule Tree towered above him, its branches glowing softly. He was drawn closer, moving as if carried by the flow of an invisible river.

The air shimmered. The bark of the tree rippled with faint light, threads of silver weaving downward into the ground, outward toward him. When they touched his boots, warmth surged up through his body.

At his feet, the snow melted away, revealing roots that coiled around his ankles and climbed higher, twining up his legs like vines. They didn't wrap around him or bind him in any way. Instead, they merged with him, drawing him into the steady, deep, ancient rhythm of the earth.

Forest life seeped into him, threading through his veins until he could sense everything. The sleeping deer in the hollow, the frozen river under its skin of ice, the hibernating bears, the insects deep underground, the sap in the trees, the very heartbeat of the mountains themselves.

And through it all, a steady presence—Holly. A thread of light winding through him. Together, entwined, their hearts beat as one.

Voices carried on the wind, faint but clear, then growing louder and layered like music. Guardian.

He awoke with a jolt, the dream lingering like breath on glass.

He sat up slowly. The fatigue was gone. His mind was clear, his body light, his senses alive in a way he couldn't explain. He could hear the creak of ice on the pond, the faint flutter of wings in the pines outside, the pulse of Al's beating heart all the way from the inn.

He was whole.

Then came the knock at his door.

UNBE-LEAF-ABLE CONNECTION

<u>Holly</u>

Holly was not one to procrastinate, yet that's exactly what she was doing. There was no excuse for not calling her father the moment she discovered the Yule Tree. However, when she arrived at the inn from the Maple Mug, she headed straight for the shower.

As warm water cascaded over her shoulders, a strange sensation washed through her. A warmth pulsed from somewhere deep inside, like an echo of the connection she'd experienced at the tree. For a moment, her vision blurred. Roots spread beneath her feet, and vines of light climbed upward, twining around her. Hearts beat together. Whispers carried in the steam. Guardian. The word came unbidden to her mind, though she couldn't say why.

She steadied herself against the shower wall, breathless, instinctively aware that these were not her thoughts, but Ivar's. Was it lingering magic or something else?

Shutting off the hot water, she blasted herself with cold, letting it shock her back to her senses. "Okay, wow. Dramatic much?" she muttered. "I'm not that special."

With efficiency, she dressed and picked up her phone, unable to procrastinate any longer. Dad would be at home, probably having dinner. She opened their private video app and called.

"Holly, darling." It was her mother. "How are things in Vermont?"

"Interesting. Are both you and Dad there? Things have taken a bit of a turn."

"How so?" her father asked, moving into the frame and joining her mother on the couch.

"Well, you're not going to believe this, but..." And so Holly explained everything. Well, not everything. She described finding what she believed to be the Yule Tree, the way it shimmered, the glow of the Yule veins. But she couldn't share what happened between her and Ivar. It was too personal. Too intimate. And she didn't think she'd find the right words.

When they wrapped things up half an hour later, the reality of the discovery was finally hitting her. She was elated, energized, almost hyper.

But what did she do now?

Her father suggested she return home as they could purchase the land remotely. Winterwood wouldn't become a new Santa site, but the Yule Tree needed protecting. Returning to NED this close to Christmas made the most logical sense. But she didn't want logic. Not yet.

There were things she needed to understand, like that hum beneath her skin and the intrinsic pull to have him close. But all that was big picture.

Tonight she needed something immediate because more energy pulsed through her than after four espressos.

She fired off a quick text to Ivar.

Holly: Ranger?

Nothing.

She tried again, but no dots and no sign that the message had been read. No need to worry; he'd had a lot to digest. But maybe she shouldn't have left him alone. What if instead of going home, he'd driven out of town, never looking back? Except if he left, she'd sense it.

Her call went straight to voice-mail.

He could be having dinner with Liv. She ran downstairs, but he wasn't there.

"I've been trying to get hold of him too," Liv said. "Poor Al wants to go home."

"I'll take him," Holly suggested. "The walk will do us both good, right, Al?" Al thumped his tail.

"I know Al will love it, but it's on the other side of town and a bit of a walk. Are you okay with that?"

"I'll be fine."

Ten minutes later, Holly was bundled up and heading out into the night, Al excited and leading the way.

The dog trotted ahead, tail high, leading her past the decorated square. Winterwood sparkled like a postcard. Every wreath tied, every candle lit, every handmade ribbon fluttering in the breeze had been made with care. This was what Christmas meant to these people. It wasn't logistics and quotas. It was love shared quietly and persistently.

A lump rose in her throat.

Al nudged her hand, pulling her from her thoughts. They'd reached Ivar's cabin. His truck was there, but all the lights were out. A knot of worry formed in her stomach. Where was he? Al let out a howl as Holly thumped on his door.

Suddenly the outside light turned on, blinding Holly as the front door burst open. Ivar stood there, blinking sleep out of his eyes, staring at Holly like he'd seen a ghost. Something in his gaze made her heart skip—a recognition, as if he'd been dreaming of her as she'd felt him in her shower.

He gave her a wry smile, but his eyes held something deeper. "Kringle. I don't have any milk and cookies, but come on in."

GETTING SPRUCED UP

<u>Ivar</u>

"So you came to see if I was okay?" he asked.

Al sat at his feet, staring up at him, head cocked in silent judgment. Ivar bent to scratch behind the dog's ears. "I didn't forget about you, buddy. I fell asleep."

Al still didn't move.

"Hey, everything's okay."

At last, Al padded to his usual spot on the couch, but his watchful eyes stayed on Ivar.

"I know you were talking to Al," Holly said from the doorway, "but is everything okay? Learning about the whole Santa and Yule Tree thing must be... a lot. I half expect- ed you to ride off into the sunset, putting as much distance between us as possible."

He gave a small chuckle. "Not that I wasn't tempted, but no. I fell asleep."

As he spoke, he absently ran a thumb along the windowsill where a small potted plant sat. The leaves seemed to lean toward his touch, unfurling slightly in the dim light. He blinked and rubbed his eyes. "Guess I'm still tired."

He watched her wring her hands, her restlessness rolling off her in waves. She was wired, holding herself together through motion, and beneath it all, he could feel her worry for him. By all rights, he should've felt the same. Instead, clarity lingered from his nap. Maybe it was the forest. Maybe it was her. Or maybe it was the miracle of sleep.

The best way to ease her tension, her energy, he decided, was with something familiar. Something simple. Like dinner.

"Why don't I make us something to eat? What time is it anyway?"

"Six thirty," she said.

"Is that all? I feel like I've lived a lifetime today."

He moved into the kitchen, filling Al's bowl. The dog's tail thumped in thanks.

Through the walls came the faint hoot of an owl, and the creak of snow-laden branches. Sounds that should have been muted by insulation and distance, yet they reached him as clearly as if his house had no walls.

He paused. "Do you hear that?"

"Hear what?"

He shook his head. "Nothing. Dinner it is, then."

"Actually," she said, "let's go out. I need to burn off some energy."

He'd rather stay home, but her nervous energy filled the small cabin. It should've been the other way around. Holly was the one used to magic, Yule veins, and flying brooms. But tonight, he was the calm one, and he'd go wherever she needed him to.

"What did you have in mind?" he asked.

"I'm not sure. This is your town. You tell me."

He smiled. "We could fly your broom to Paris."

"No way. Expecting me to watch you throw up for a third time in one day is asking a bit much, don't you think?"

Their shared laughter softened the moment, and an understanding passed between them like a current. They were in this together.

And as the tension eased from her shoulders, something inside him settled too—like a missing piece falling into place.

QUIZMAS EVE

<u>Holly</u>

The Sugarhouse Brewery glowed like a hearth against the snow. Warm amber lights gleamed through its tall windows, throwing gold across the frosted glass. Inside, the air was thick with laughter, roasted garlic, and the faint sweetness of maple sugar.

Holly shrugged off her coat and followed Ivar toward a booth in the corner.

He slid into one side. She took the other.

"No snowshoes. No maps. No brooms," she said, resting her elbows on the table. "Feels almost like a normal evening."

Ivar grinned. "Speak for yourself."

"Actually, I'm not really," she said, but the corners of her mouth tugged up. "Normal for me is a microwaved burrito for dinner and then a couple of hours of work before bed."

"That's not what I imagined #SantaLife to be like. Not that I ever thought about it."

She laughed softly, the sound surprising even her. Being with Ivar was easy—too easy.

Before she could reply, a server appeared beside their table. She had thick auburn hair in a messy braid, a flannel shirt rolled to the elbows, and a pencil tucked behind one ear. Her name tag read Tess.

"Evening, Ivar," she said. "Didn't expect to see you out on trivia night. Who's your friend?"

"This is Holly Kringle," Ivar said. "Holly, this is Tess. Winterwood's brewmaster number one."

"Ah," Tess said with a smile, turning to Holly. "So you're the one looking at the Hale land."

"I am," Holly said. "Nice to meet you. What do you recommend on a night like this?"

"Well, the Irish stew will thaw your bones. And I'd pair it with our winter cider—maple-spiced with a hint of cinnamon."

"Sold," Holly said.

"I'll have the same," Ivar added. "And a pint of my usual."

"Coming right up," Tess said, scribbling on her pad. "Better hurry, trivia's starting soon."

"What does she mean by that?" Holly asked.

"I'm not much of a trivia guy. I haven't been to one since I moved back."

"You're kidding."

"Nope. What about you? Is trivia big in the North Pole?"

"I do not live at the North Pole. I live in NED. It stands for the Northeast Division. And I have no idea whether trivia is big or not. So what's your usual?"

"Imperial stout."

"Of course," she said with mock solemnity. "But I kind of pegged you as a maple IPA kind of guy."

"And that means what exactly?"

"You've got a very I'm from Vermont kind of vibe, that's all."

He smirked. "You and your vibes."

"Yes, well, right now my vibe wants to ask you about California. Because that doesn't seem to suit your vibe."

Ivar hesitated, then exhaled. "Yeah. Well. That was a lifetime ago, or so it seems. I studied programming at college, wanting to go into gaming. We were a small start-up with big plans. The hours were long. The pace was fast, and the deadlines were approaching. My girlfriend at the time was the lead designer. We lived and breathed code."

Holly nodded, watching him closely.

"Then I collapsed one day in the parking lot," he said. "Stress-induced heart arrhythmia. That's what the doctors called it."

"Oh my goodness," she said softly. "What happened?"

"I spent a few days in the hospital, and for the first time in years, I didn't open my laptop even though Cynthia had dropped it off. And when I finally walked out of there—this sounds ridiculous—a cardinal dropped a small pine branch on my windshield, and all I could think of was returning here."

She blinked. "That's oddly specific."

"You're right. It felt like a sign, so I listened. It made me realize I didn't want to spend the rest of my life behind a screen, and I literally packed up my car that day, knowing I had to return here." He rubbed the back of his neck. "When I told Cynthia I wanted out, she laughed, assuming it was a phase because of the collapse. After a couple of weeks, when she realized I was serious and staying in Winterwood, she got angry and took our prototype to a competitor before I could sign over my half."

Holly winced. "Ouch."

"I lost everything," he said. Then, with a small shrug: "But I was where I belonged. Want to know what's even stranger?" He leaned forward, and she did too.

"A cardinal dropped a pine branch on my windshield a few weeks ago."

Her eyes widened. "You're kidding."

"Nope. And then you show up and we find the tree."

For a moment, neither spoke. Their eyes held over the candle flickering between them.

"Do you think—" Holly began, but then Tess returned with their drinks.

"Here you go. One stout. One winter cider. The stew'll be out in five."

"To surviving broom travel," Ivar said, raising his glass, as Tess walked away.

"And to not vomiting on your copilot," Holly added, clinking gently.

The bell over the bar rang three times.

"All right, folks," called George Keating, the town's unofficial trivia master, from behind the microphone. "Teams of two to four!"

A cheer rose from the crowd. Emma waved from the next booth over. "Ivar, I can't believe you're here. You're joining, right? You too, Holly! Newcomers always bring luck."

"Oh, come on, Emma," Ivar groaned good-naturedly. "You know I'm not up for this."

"That's why you need me," Emma teased. "Our team's called The Maple Mug Misfits!"

Liv appeared then, wearing a smile and sliding into Emma's booth. A mug of cider awaited her. "Join us, Ivar. That way if we lose, I can blame you."

"You always do," Ivar said.

Holly looked between them, amused. "You people take this seriously."

Tess passed by, dropping off their bowls of stew. "Oh, honey," she said, grinning. "In Winterwood, trivia night is blood sport."

"In honor of the upcoming Winterwood Christmas Carnival," George called out, "tonight's theme is Holiday History and Folklore!"

Ivar shot Holly a conspiratorial smile. "Actually, Emma. I think we'll join you after all."

The next hour flew by in a whirl of laughter, music, and shouted answers.

Holly found herself leaning over the table, arguing about whether Dasher or Dancer was older (George ruled for Dancer, and although he was wrong, Holly let it go). She knew more than she thought, considering she'd never given much attention to tradition or folklore. Of course, she didn't know much about the local traditions, but she found herself listening with genuine interest to the stories and the gentle nostalgia threaded through every laugh and memory shared around the table.

Between rounds, she and Ivar exchanged grins over their mugs. Each time he laughed, it reverberated inside her, thawing something that had been frozen far too long.

There was a spark woven through their connection. She wasn't sure what it meant, but she wanted to stay in it, to enjoy being seen and understood. To have fun.

By the final question, everyone was leaning forward. It was a close race, and this question was worth extra points. "What traditional holiday figure rides a broomstick on the eve of Epiphany?" George read aloud.

The bar went quiet. Holly froze, her pulse quickening.

Then Ivar's slow, wicked grin spread across his face. "I got this."

He stood, and while his voice boomed across the room, his eyes never left hers. "La Befana."

"Correct!" George shouted. Cheers and friendly boos erupted around them.

Liv and Emma clapped, Tess banged a spoon against the bar, and Ivar raised his glass again. "To the Maple Mug Misfits," he said, "and all the Christmas figures out there."

He held his hand up to Holly for a high five. She laughed, accepting congratulations from some of the other teams, like she belonged there.

With him.

Ivar

The night air hit like a cool cloth after the warmth of the brewery. Snow had started again. Big soft flakes spiraled through the street-lamps, landing in Holly's hair like bits of starlight. She pulled her scarf tighter, her cheeks flushed from cider and laughter.

"I can't believe we actually won," she said, glancing over at him.

"Pretty sure that means I retire undefeated," he said. "Go out on top."

"Coward."

"Strategic," he corrected, hands tucked in his coat pockets. "I'd rather stay a legend than risk humiliation next week."

She gave him a sideways smile. "You liked it."

"A bit," he admitted. "But don't tell anyone. I've got a reputation as a recluse to maintain."

"Too late," she said, bumping his shoulder lightly. "You laughed out loud and high-fived half the bar after our victory."

"That was an accident."

They both chuckled, their boots crunching on the snow. The town had quieted, with only the faint glow of windows and the scent of wood smoke lingering in the air.

Holly stopped for a moment, taking it in. "It's beautiful here."

He looked at her, the lamplight soft on her face, and thought the same thing.

He'd spent years keeping to himself, convinced solitude was easier. Trivia nights, crowded rooms, small talk was all noise. He'd chosen silence instead.

But tonight had been different.

Because of her.

And not for the mind-altering introduction to a world of magic. Something simpler, but equally profound. He'd forgotten the joy of sharing a laugh, of having a partner—not in work, not in survival, but in living.

"Thank you," she said suddenly.

"For what?"

"For today. For reminding me of how to have fun."

He smiled, shy but warm. "You make a pretty good trivia partner."

"Don't get used to it."

"I'll take my chances."

They reached the steps of the inn, hesitation hanging between them. For a moment, neither of them moved. The air between them felt charged again, but not with magic. Something quieter and human. The temptation to close the distance, to lean in and kiss her, was strong.

But whatever had stirred beneath the trees still lingered between them, and it deserved time to take root.

"Good night, Holly."

"Good night, Ivar."

The door closed, and for a long moment, he simply stood there, feeling that same earthly hum of peace, life, and promise.

Holly

Later, lying in bed, Holly stared up at the ceiling, the day looping through her mind in flashes. Her thoughts spun, circling back to one thing. One person.

Ivar.

After all that had happened, it was Ivar who grounded them. Who grounded her. Tonight at the brewery, she'd been a version of herself who laughed and teased. Holly the person, not Holly the Santa.

Her phone buzzed on the nightstand. The screen lit up.

Ivar Nilsen.

She smiled before she even opened it.

Ivar: Trivia champ still awake?
Holly: Just taking my victory lap.
Ivar: Pretty sure I carried the team.
Holly: You answered one question.
Ivar: It was the winning question.
  That counts for at least five.
Holly: Technically true. And fine,
  partial hero status granted.
Ivar: I'll take it.
(pause)

Ivar: Thanks for today, Kringle. All
  of it.
Holly: Same, Ranger. Same.

21
days until
Christmas Eve

TASKING THROUGH THE SNOW

<u>Holly</u>

Holly's phone buzzed for the fifth time in the last minute.

She set her coffee mug down, squinting at the screen: a string of messages from her brothers, her sister, one from Rita full of exclamation points, and a terse <u>Call me when you can</u> from her father.

News about the Yule Tree had apparently spread.

She'd expected excitement. What she hadn't expected (read: wanted) was the avalanche of follow-up questions.

When her phone buzzed again, she slid it facedown on the table and switched it to silent.

Just for a few minutes.

"Morning, sunshine!" Liv called from behind the buffet table, wielding a coffee pot like a scepter of joy. "You're practically glowing."

"It's your delicious pastries."

"Uh-huh." Liv's grin widened. "You mean it's not from our victory last night?"

Holly ducked her head, pretending to fuss with her napkin. "Pure luck. I just happened to know a few Christmas facts."

Liv topped up her cup of coffee. "A few? You were like a one-woman holiday encyclopedia. Even George looked impressed."

"I may have taken a folklore course in college," Holly said, wrapping both hands around her mug and enjoying the heat.

Liv arched a brow. "A folklore course, huh? Interesting. Seems like fate that you'd end up in Winterwood, then."

"Fate's a strong word," Holly said lightly.

Liv leaned against the counter, her eyes twinkling. "Ivar also mentioned you might be sticking around a little longer than expected. Said something about your family moving ahead with the Hale land purchase?"

"Yes," Holly said, careful to sound neutral. "That's the plan."

"Well, that's fantastic news." Liv's smile brightened even further. "And since you'll be around..." She hesitated. "Will you please, please, please help with the Carnival?"

"The Carnival?" Holly echoed.

"Yes. You organized that festival timeline like an angel descended from the North Pole. Everything's running smoother than ever, but I could really use your help on-site today."

Holly's first instinct was panic. "On-site? As in... outdoors?"

Liv nodded cheerfully. "Exactly. Hanging banners, setting up booths, that sort of thing."

"I'm not sure that's where my strengths lie," Holly said carefully. "I'm more of a—"

"Spreadsheet girl," Liv finished for her. "I know. But George usually helps with the banners, and he twisted his ankle leaving trivia last night. I can't do it, and

Tess is short-staffed at the brewery. Please?"

Holly searched for a graceful escape route, but the little Kringle voice in her head—the one that sounded suspiciously like her grandfather—reminded her that Kringles help bring Christmas cheer wherever it's needed.

"It wouldn't hurt to keep busy, I suppose." If she was staying in Winterwood, she might as well be useful.

Liv's grin was triumphant. "Perfect! I'll have Ivar pick you up in an hour."

Holly's mug paused mid-sip. "Ivar?"

"Well, yes. He's been volunteered to help too," Liv said innocently. "He's got the ladder, the truck, and the muscle. And between the two of you, I'm confident the square will be sparkling in no time."

Holly suspected there was more matchmaking than management behind this plan, but she couldn't bring herself to protest.

"A morning with Ivar," she said, mostly to herself, "sounds... productive."

Liv didn't even bother hiding her grin. "That's one word for it."

NO ELFING WAY

<u>Holly</u>

Holly stood beside Ivar's truck, craning her neck toward the enormous banner in his arms.

"Welcome to Winterwood's Christmas Carnival," she read aloud. "That looks heavy."

"Only if you're not a big, strong park ranger like me," he said, flashing her a grin.

"Well, I guess you don't need me, then."

Ivar chuckled and climbed the ladder, the banner draped over one shoulder. "You're in charge of keeping your end from touching the ground."

"I can handle that," Holly said, tugging her mittens tighter. She lifted the bottom edge, then promptly lost her balance when the wind caught it like a sail.

"Careful!" Ivar called, steadying the rope from above.

"I'm fine!" she said, even as the banner whipped against her like an angry flag. "I just didn't expect aerodynamics to be part of the job description."

A familiar voice piped up from a nearby bench. "You've got to anchor the corners, young lady!"

Holly turned to see George Keating, leg wrapped in a bulky brace, waving a cane like a conductor's baton.

"I thought you were supposed to be resting, George," Ivar said, halfway up the ladder.

"Supervising," George corrected. "I've got decades of banner expertise. Someone's got to make sure you don't hang it crooked like last year."

"It was straight," Ivar said.

"Not from where I was sitting."

"You were sitting at the brewery."

"Best vantage point in town." George winked.

Holly laughed. "Should we take his advice?"

"Absolutely not," Ivar said. "If we do, the banner will be upside down by noon."

"I heard that!" George hollered.

Holly grinned up at Ivar. "You two seem to have a history."

"Small town," he said. "Everyone's got history."

Ivar tugged the rope taut. "Hold steady. Almost there."

The banner fluttered once more before falling neatly into place across Main Street, its red letters gleaming against the gray sky.

They stepped back together, side by side, admiring their handi-work.

"Perfect," Holly said, brushing snow off her coat.

"Not bad for Spreadsheet Holly," Ivar teased.

"Careful," she said. "I might start adding event management to my resume."

"Pretty soon you'll be running the whole carnival."

"Don't tempt me."

A cheer echoed from across the square, where Emma and Tess were hauling out boxes of ornaments and garland. Emma cupped her hands around her mouth. "Looks amazing! Holly, you're hired!"

"I'll send you an invoice!" Holly called back, laughing.

"Good luck getting paid!" Tess shouted.

George thumped his cane approvingly. "Straight enough! Could be a bit tighter, but I'll allow it."

Ivar rolled his eyes. "You should really take up a hobby, George."

"This is my hobby."

Holly smiled, feeling remarkably at home.

The illusion shattered when her phone rang. It was Rita. "I better get this," she said to Ivar. "I've been avoiding them all morning."

"Hi Rita. Is everything okay?"

"I'm calling to ask you the same thing. I haven't heard from you all morning. And I know you're not out in the wilderness. Your father told me about the you-know-what. Is it true?"

She cast a glance at Ivar, who was trying to untangle a set of lights. "I believe so."

"That's incredible."

"Kringle, let's go. I need your help," Ivar called out, holding the lights up in defeat.

"Kringle?" Rita asked.

"Can I call you back at another time? I'm helping set up for the Winterwood Christmas Carnival while I wait for updates on the land purchase."

"You're what? Wait. Are you being... social?"

"Don't sound so shocked. Spreading Christmas cheer and goodwill is part of the job description."

"Well, whatever it is, it sounds a lot like fun. I'll leave you to it," Rita said, and Holly could hear the smile in her voice as she hung up.

"Everything okay?" Ivar asked.

"It is." Holly slipped her phone into her coat pocket and realized, with surprise, that she hadn't asked for NED updates.

"Good. How about we warm up with a hot chocolate and a scone? Or perhaps you'd prefer hot milk and cookies? Emma has some sugar cookies in the shape of reindeer."

"You're a funny man, Mr. Park Ranger. Be careful, or I'll put you on the naughty list."

"The naughty list. Are you saying that there's..." He held up a hand. "No. Don't tell me. I don't want to know."

"Suit yourself, but if those binoculars you want don't end up under the tree, you'll be sorry."

He stopped dead in his tracks. "How'd you know I wanted binoculars for Christmas?"

"Relax. I saw you looking at some on your phone."

"Of course, I mean... I didn't really believe that..." He held the cafe door open.

"You make this too easy," she teased, walking past him into the Maple Mug.

Ivar placed the order while Holly found a table by the fire. He arrived carrying a plate and two forks.

"It's a maple cranberry tart. We can share."

"You folks never get tired of maple?"

"Bite your tongue." He held out his arm, rolling up his sleeve. "See these veins? Pure maple syrup."

She laughed and brushed her fingers against his arm. That unforgettable, tingly warmth spread up her arm. She gently withdrew her hand, wondering if he felt it too, though she wasn't quite brave enough to meet his eyes.

Ivar

"There you go, enjoy," the server said, placing their drinks on the table.

"This place is dangerously comforting," Holly said, stirring her foam. "If I lived here, I'd never get any work done."

Ivar smiled, the heat from her touch still radiating up his arm. It was cute, the way she'd blushed, so he knew she'd felt it too. "Your work ethic is too strong, but I'd like to see you try."

She opened her mouth to reply, but the bell over the door jingled so sharply that half the cafe glanced up.

Gwen Brooks swept in, cheeks flushed from the cold, a red scarf trailing behind her like a warning flag. She didn't bother removing her gloves before striding straight toward their table.

"Ivar," she said, slightly out of breath, "mind if I sit for a moment?"

He straightened, instantly wary. "Sure, Gwen. This is Holly Kringle. She's with the family interested in the Hale land."

Gwen nodded briskly and offered her hand across the table. "Nice to meet you, Ms. Kringle. I was actually just on the phone with an Adam Kringle not ten minutes ago."

Holly blinked. "My father."

"Right. Well, I'll tell you both what I told him." Gwen dropped into the empty chair, leaning forward, her expression grave. "Rowan Hale's brother, Chad, has decided to get involved. And apparently, he's managed to convince her not to sell."

"So she's pulling out?" Ivar asked.

"Worse," Gwen said. "Chad's put to-gether a whole business plan. He wants to develop the land him-self—a ski resort and spa. Says it'll 'modernize' Winterwood and 'bring in tourism dollars.'" She air-quoted the words.

Ivar's hands curled around his mug. "I checked recently. That land isn't zoned for that kind of develop-ment."

"Not yet," Gwen said. "But Chad's persuasive. He's already talking about investors and infrastructure grants. He's got big-city energy and, apparently, enough charm to match. And Ivar, I'm sorry, but if this goes through... we'll lose ac-cess to the trail network."

The words hit like a gust of cold air. Ivar's pulse quickened, and for a split second, he could swear he heard the forest—the deep creak of branches, the moaning of ice under stress. A pressure built be-hind his ribs, sharp and protec-tive, as if the land itself was calling out in protest.

"No commission for me," Gwen added with a humorless laugh. "And a lot of angry townsfolk once the bulldozers roll in. Anyway..." She stood, pulling her scarf tight. "Sorry to be the bearer of bad tid-ings. Ms. Kringle, lovely to meet you. Though I suppose there's no deal to be made now."

And with that, she was gone—the door jingling behind her, letting in a swirl of cold before it shut again.

Silence filled the space between them. The cheerful buzz of the cafe felt suddenly distant, muffled by the weight of what Gwen had said.

Holly stared at the table, her latte cooling untouched.

Ivar exhaled hard, running a hand through his hair. "A ski resort. On that land." He shook his head.

"Holly," he said softly, but with clear determination. "We can't let him destroy the forest, the tree."

"Then we don't."

DECK THE HALES

<u>Holly</u>

The buzz of the Maple Mug faded into a dull hum as Holly pulled her tablet from her purse and set it between the mugs. The glow of the screen was harsh compared to the honeyed light of the cafe.

"You keep your tablet with you at all times?" Ivar asked.

"Yes. You never know when you might need it, and I believe this is one of those times."

"You got me there," he said.

"Okay," she said, channeling all her strategic planning skills. "Ideas."

Ivar leaned forward, elbows on the table. "Town hall meeting. The city council needs to get involved right away."

"Good," Holly said, typing fast. "But Chad Hale's group will argue it's good for the town, bringing in jobs, tourism, and growth."

"I've already looked into similar projects," Ivar said, rubbing his thumb along the rim of his mug. "When it first went up for sale, I wanted to be prepared. The land's too far out of town; people won't drive into Winterwood. They'll stay at the resort, eat there, shop there, ski there. A few budget travelers will come into town, but it won't make up for the traffic or the environmental damage."

"Perfect," Holly murmured, her fingers flying across the tablet screen. "We'll compile that into a brief listing economic losses, environmental impact, and anything else we can think of."

"We already talked about zoning."

"If there's a loophole, Chad Hale will find it."

Her phone buzzed on the table. <u>Dad</u> flashed across the screen.

Dad: Just heard from a Gwen
  Brooks.
Holly: Me too.
Dad: If that is indeed the Yule Tree,
  we must do everything we can to
  protect that land.
Holly: We're already working on a
  plan.
Dad: We?
Holly: Ivar Nilsen. Park Ranger. Call
  you later.

She hesitated, thumb hovering over the screen. Then she opened another thread.

Holly: Rita, I need you to research Rowan and Chad Hale. Start with property records, permits, business filings—everything. And dig up anything on Betty Hale and the whole family history. My father can fill you in if he hasn't already.

She slipped the phone back into her bag. "I'm getting us help," she said.

Ivar tilted his head. "Magical help? Because I'd take a Christmas miracle about now."

"No," she said with a small, determined smile. "Research help. The next best thing. We need to know everything about this project. What if..." she hesitated. "What if I go in posing as an investor?"

His brows lifted. "As in?"

"As in someone who's interested in funding the resort. I could get access to details and see what he's really up to."

Ivar considered it, eyes narrowing slightly as he leaned back in his chair. "Not bad, Kringle. Not bad," he said slowly. "We could say you had the same idea for the land, and you still want in. He'll talk to you."

Holly nodded. "Exactly."

"It might upset some folks around here," he said gently. "Liv, Emma, Eli, if they think you've changed sides."

"I know," she said quietly. "But if it saves the land… it's worth it. They'll understand eventually."

Ivar studied her, something soft flickering behind his eyes.

"Then we do this together," he said finally. "For the forest. For Winterwood. For the Yule Tree."

Holly met his gaze, the world narrowing to the small table between them. Sitting there with Ivar, surrounded by laughter and a town that celebrated the joy of giving, she realized that the Yule power fading wasn't just a logistics issue for the Santas. It went beyond hidden villages and sleigh routes. This was about what Christmas truly meant.

"For the spirit of Christmas," she said.

20
days until
Christmas Eve

MISTLE-NOPE

<u>Holly</u>

The hotel lobby smelled of polished wood and flavored coffee, with faux-fur throws draped over the backs of sleek leather armchairs. It was the kind of place where holiday music played softly, but the cheer was curated. Not unlike Holly's office back home come December.

After a quick glance at her reflection in the glass door, she pushed it open, and stepped into the lounge. Near the fire, two people sat at a low table scattered with brochures. She recognized Chale Hale immediately, even without an introduction.

He looked every inch the investor he claimed to be, with his clean-cut, charismatic, and a little too polished appearance.

The woman beside him stood when she approached, offering a warm, but slightly guarded smile. "Ms. Kringle. Thanks for coming. I'm Rowan Hale, and this is my brother, Chad."

"Holly please. And thanks for making time," Holly said, shaking Rowan's hand.

"Holly Kringle. Such an interesting name," Chad said, gesturing for them to sit. "We would have assumed you were a crank call had Gwen Brooks not contacted us on your behalf."

"Yes, I get that a lot," Holly said, taking a seat.

"We're glad you reached out. As you must know, the development scene in this region is about to blow up. I mean, why else would you be here? We both know it's the perfect time to get in early."

"We're certainly interested. Walk me through your vision," she said, folding her hands neatly on the table.

Chad launched into the presentation. It was smooth. Practiced.

"We're talking twenty to thirty luxury cabins at phase one. Gondola access to the ridge. There will be year-round appeal with fall foliage in the autumn, skiing in the winter, and mountain biking in the summer. Not to mention our wellness retreats with influencer-ready aesthetics. I've got early interest from

two hotel chains and a recreation-
al outfitter brand."

He swiped through renderings of
gleaming timber lodges, firepits
with glass walls, heated pools
open all year, saunas, and hot
tubs. "Restaurants, bars, shop-
ping, you name it." Chad scrolled
to another rendering. "Winterwood's got charm, sure. But it's
sleepy. This development would
bring jobs, tourism, and a serious
bump in property values."

Rowan looked tense and unsure
the entire time. Clearly not comfortable with what her brother
was selling.

"And the land itself?" Holly asked,
feigning casual interest. "I'm not
sure the town of Winterwood is
even as big as what you're propos-
ing. Is the land large enough to
handle a development of this size?

What about environmental consid-
erations?"

Chad waved a hand. "There are
more than enough forests in Vermont. People romanticize nature,
but this way they can enjoy it without, you know... actually being in
it."

Rowan's brow twitched, but she
said nothing.

"And the town?" Holly pressed.
"How have they responded?"

Chad shrugged. "We anticipate
some pushback, but we'll host a
town hall at some point and convince them to see it our way. People always resist change at first.
They'll come around once they see
what's in it for them."

Rowan finally spoke. "We need to
be careful not to alienate people.
This isn't just land. It's history, and
it's their home."

Chad smiled, charming but dismissive. "People move on, or they move away. That's what progress is. There are worse things than moving. Look at us. We moved all the time. We never had a hometown, and we turned out fine. People are nostalgic for something that doesn't exist anymore."

Holly stood. "Well, thank you, Chad, Rowan. This has been very informative. I'll take a few of your brochures to share with my family. We'll be in touch soon." She held out her hand and shook theirs. A plan, already forming in her mind.

Holly was exiting the hotel when her phone buzzed with a text.

Rita: Chad and Rowan Hale. Parents passed away young (car accident). Kids grew up in boarding schools. No hometown. No community roots. Rowan spent several summers in Winterwood with her aunt. Chad (seven years older) didn't. Spent summers at camps: sailing, hockey, horseback riding, etc. Betty Hale lived there all her life. Married once, but widowed at a young age. No children. Land goes back generations.

"So," Ivar said as Holly climbed into his truck. "How did it go?"

She handed him the brochures.

He whistled. "This is bigger than we thought. He doesn't care if the whole valley gets clear-cut."

Holly nodded. "No. But Rowan might. She's not as sold on this.

And, this is going to sound weird, but Chad seems to hate the forest on a personal level. I also received some information from Rita." She explained the Hale's background.

He glanced at her. "What are you thinking?"

She smiled slowly. "We make them care. We show them what they've never had."

"You mean a hometown? Community?"

"Exactly."

"And you think that will be enough?"

"It's a start."

Ivar gave a dry chuckle. "You're planning to save the forest and pull off a Christmas movie arc with them?"

"You say that like it's hard. Remember, I'm a Kringle. But we will need help."

"And who would that be?"

She gave him a grin. "Why, the Christmas Carnival Committee, of course."

He shook his head. "You really are going to Christmas-movie the heck out of this thing, aren't you? And before you say anything, yes, I know. You're a Kringle."

SANTA'S LITTLE PLAN

<u>Ivar</u>

Marty, Tess's brother, led Holly and Ivar to the brewery's backroom. "Right back with a stout and a cider," he said, already disappearing through the swinging doors.

Ivar noticed that the room buzzed with the quiet ease of friends who'd known one another forever. His sister was hunched over a stack of Carnival flyers, muttering about printer ink. Tess perched on a keg, twisting a candy cane between her fingers like a wand. Emma leaned against the wall beside the coat rack, scarf still around her neck, cheeks pink from the cold.

"Look at you," Tess said, grinning at Holly. "Already in your unofficial Winterwood uniform of flannel shirt, sweater, and snow boots."

"Just trying to blend in," Holly joked.

"Good luck with that," Emma teased. "You've got 'project manager' written all over you."

Liv smiled without looking up. "If she's volunteering for the Carnival, I'll take her."

"So what's this all about?" Marty asked, placing the drinks on the table. "We're busy tonight. I don't have much time to spare."

"Well, then. Let's get down to business," Ivar said, setting the brochures on the table. "It's about

Chad Hale's proposed development."

Word had spread quickly that he wanted to build a resort, but even the most pessimistic among them would not have anticipated how severely the Hale project would change the landscape.

"Surely this would never clear the environmental assessment," Tess said.

Ivar glanced at Holly. "We have people looking into it, but don't for-get, they do too. Same with road capacity, electricity usage, water requirements. You name it, we've got someone working on it." Sure, they were at some mysterious hidden village somewhere in the world, but he'd keep that between him and Holly.

"What about the sister? Doesn't she own the land?" Liv asked.

"She does, and for the time being she's going along with it."

"So, what's the plan?" Marty asked.

Ivar moved behind Holly and placed his hands on her shoulders. "Holly and I want them to fall in love with Winterwood," Ivar announced. "By giving them something they've never had—a real hometown. Somewhere they belong." He anticipated that the room would fall silent in disbelief. It did.

"That's not much of a plan," Emma finally said.

"Yes. And I thought Miss Kringle wanted to buy the land. How can we be certain that this isn't a ploy for us to sabotage the land sale so she can buy it and develop it herself?" Marty asked.

"A fair question," Holly answered. "Yes, my family wants to buy the land, but our goal is to preserve and protect the forest. Not exploit it."

"How do we know we can trust her, Ivar?" Tess asked.

"Because I trust her, and you know how much the forest means to me," Ivar replied. The room fell silent once again.

"That's good enough for me," Liv said.

"Then that's good enough for us too," Tess said with only a hint of reluctance. "Perhaps if we had more details."

"The Hales think they are going to get resistance from the town," Ivar began. "So, let's do the opposite. Let's be kind and welcoming. Starting with the Christmas Carnival. We'll make them grand marshals."

"Aren't grand marshals for parades?" Marty asked.

"You know what I mean."

"By being involved, they become part of the town," Holly said. "We'll have them judge some of the events, so that they're not ob-servers; they're participants. The town will begin to mean something to them, and they'll care about what happens to it."

Liv looked thoughtful. "That's clever. They'd have to mingle, talk to people, get to know us."

"And," Holly said, "it's public enough to make them feel hon-ored, especially Chad. He struck me as the kind of person who would enjoy that."

Ivar added, "Neither child had a hometown growing up. If they feel like they belong here–"

"—they might want to protect it," Holly finished, their eyes meeting briefly.

There was a beat of silence, then Liv nodded. "I'll draft the official invite. Emma, can you bake something that says 'Welcome to Winterwood'—but with sprinkles?"

Emma beamed. "Sprinkles are my love language."

"Done," Liv said. "Let's turn this Christmas Carnival into a charm offensive."

19
days until
Christmas Eve

SECRET SANTA CONNECTION

<u>Holly</u>

All that talk about home at the meeting the night before had left Holly curious about Betty Hale's house. Maybe seeing it would help them understand the Hales better, or even give them a clue about what might make the siblings feel more welcome.

So, the next morning, she called Chad to ask if she could stop by. If he was surprised about her interest in the main property, he didn't show it, too eager to secure her investment to question her motives.

And now, as the truck wheels crunched through the snow of the uncleared driveway, Holly found herself both excited and uneasy about what they might find.

"Maybe broom travel would have been easier," she quipped when the tires spun on a patch of ice.

"Maybe it followed us here," Ivar replied.

"When I left the inn, it was curled up in front of the fire with a coffee and a good book."

He raised his eyebrows. "Tell me you're joking."

"Of course I'm joking. It seems to have gone back to its regular dormant-broomy self."

"Is it strange that this conversation doesn't strike me as weird?"

Holly laughed as Ivar turned off the engine.

Silence settled around them as they glanced around the property. The house stood at the end of the drive, a weatherworn two-story with faded blue shutters, stoic and empty but not unloved. The shed off to the side leaned slightly, as if bowing under the weight of its secrets.

For a moment, neither spoke. A faint current of energy hummed in the air; it was subtle but also too strong to ignore. Both of them shivered at the same instant, and when she turned to Ivar, he was already looking at her. No words passed between them, but a quiet understanding did. Whatever that was, they'd both felt it.

A crunching sound came from behind, and they turned to see an SUV pulling up the drive. Chad stepped out, sunglasses on despite the overcast sky.

Holly and Ivar walked to meet him as Rowan climbed out of the passenger seat. "Ivar is the local park ranger," Holly said, introducing him. "He's been consulting with me as I assess the land. I brought him along today for a second opinion, if that's all right."

"Of course," Chad said, though his tone suggested otherwise.

"And you're planning to tear down the buildings?" Holly asked.

"Yes," he replied briskly. "I've brought the plans to show you."

Rowan said nothing, eyes fixed on the ground.

"They must be over a hundred years old," Holly said, studying the weathered siding and faded shutters. "Do you mind if I take a peek inside? I love old houses."

"There's not much to see," Chad began, but Rowan's face brightened, and she was already moving toward the porch.

"It hasn't changed much," Rowan said softly, running her gloved fingers along the railing. "Aunt Betty loved this place. She said that the quiet helped her think."

"Did you ever come out here?" Holly asked Ivar quietly as he fell into step beside her.

He shook his head. "No. Not many people did. Everyone said Miss Hale was eccentric, but kind."

Rowan turned the key in the old brass lock, the sound loud in the stillness. "Come on in."

Inside, the air was cool and a little stagnant, but clean, carrying the faint scent of cedar, mothballs, and old paper. Light filtered through lace curtains, and the old floorboards creaked under their boots.

"It's smaller than I remember," Rowan said, her voice drifting ahead of them. "But I was smaller then, too." She trailed her fingers across the top of a sideboard cluttered with glass jars and yellowed recipe cards. "But Aunt Betty always said that small houses have big hearts."

Holly smiled faintly. "That's a lovely sentiment."

The living room opened on their left. Holly took in the floral wallpaper, brick hearth, and shelves of books that bowed under their weight. There was nothing remarkable about it. Just a sense of a life well-lived, of evenings spent by the fire, and of mornings with coffee and a hearty breakfast.

Chad lingered in the doorway, scrolling on his phone. "You see what I mean," he said. "Nothing special."

"Chad," Rowan admonished. "This is our family history."

"Whatever," Chad replied.

Holly ignored him, focusing on Rowan as she took in the crocheted afghan on the sofa, the framed photographs of maple harvests and winter carnivals.

"Have you not been here recently?" Holly asked.

"Not for years. I kept in touch with Aunt Betty through letters and then emails, but I'm ashamed to say I never came here. Life seemed to get in the way. I regret that now."

They moved through the rest of the house. Through the kitchen and pantry before climbing the narrow stairs leading to two small bedrooms. Holly noted the slant of the ceilings, the uneven floor, the nail in the wall where a picture used to hang. It was a home that had once been full of love.

"What will you do with all these items and family mementos?" Holly asked.

"If Chad had his way, we'd bulldoze the whole thing. But I'll go through it. There are some things worthy of a local museum. Some things I'll keep."

As they made their way to the door, disappointment crept in. Nothing Holly had seen brought them any closer to understanding the Hales.

"There's something else you should see," Rowan said, her tone a bit brighter. "I spent a lot of time there each summer."

They followed Rowan around the side of the house toward the shed. Holly's eyes landed on the weathered door. On it hung a rusted bell from a green ribbon. She stopped as a tremor of recognition moved through her.

Rowan smiled wistfully. "She kept that up all year, saying, 'A little Christmas magic keeps out the wrong kind of mischief.'" Then she pulled the door open, and they peered inside. "I used to help her polish little wooden toys in here during summer visits. She'd hum these tunes I didn't know and make me paint stars on everything."

This time, Holly went pale.

Ivar turned toward her. "You okay?"

Holly forced a smile. "Just taking it in."

But she could tell he didn't believe her. And he was right. She wasn't just taking it in. She'd realized the Hales weren't living near a Yule vein by chance. They knew something. About magic. About Kringles. The shed was full of signs.

Chad stepped up to the shed, peering in as if it were a closet of junk. "Can't wait to bulldoze this, either." He wiped the snow off an old picnic table, laying out his construction plans. "Imagine all this gone," he waved at the buildings and the forest before pointing. "Hotel there, village there. Shops and restaurants underneath. Condos on top. Parking to your left. The gondola takes you up. It's quite a ride, but then you're in the ski bowl."

Ivar peered at the map.

"Holly, take a look at this," he said, pointing at the ski bowl.

She leaned over the map, pulse quickening as her gaze followed Ivar's finger. The exact center of the ski bowl was also the location of the Yule Tree.

Her stomach flipped. Panic wasn't in her vocabulary, but the world tilted, her body remembering the same dizzy surge she'd experienced the day Rita called the medic.

But then, Ivar's shoulder brushed against hers. His presence steadied her, like roots anchoring a tree against strong winds. Her heart still raced, but the world stopped spinning quite so violently. As she turned to move, her foot slipped slightly on a patch of ice.

Before she could fall, Ivar reached out and caught her elbow. Reflexively, she grabbed his hand.

She didn't let go.

Neither did he.

Their fingers interlaced natural-ly, like puzzle pieces finding their match. A warmth traveled up her arm that had nothing to do with temperature, but it also wasn't Yule Tree energy. This was from her heart.

Their eyes met. His were steady and soft as they held her in his gaze, and she wondered if he knew how her heart stuttered as he looked at her that way.

He cleared his throat. "Don't wor-ry," he said, voice low. "I got you. But I think it's time to go."

Beside them, Chad scowled at the trees. "Good idea. This place gives me the creeps. Let's wrap this up."

Holly's head was whirling. She had come hoping to learn about Rowan's emotional connection to the property. Instead, it was as

if someone had dumped a puzzle onto her lap and expected her
to put it together without showing
her the picture on the box.

It wasn't until they reached Ivar's
truck that she released his hand.

"Thank you," she said.

"What happened? I thought you
were going to faint."

"Me too," she admitted, allowing
him to help her up. They waved
as the Hales drove off, and even
though they were alone, she waited until he was inside the truck and
the doors were closed to tell him
what she suspected.

"The Hales," she said. "They're from
my world. The bell on the door,
the wooden toys, and probably
the tunes Rowan didn't recognize.
They're traditions, older, sure, but
we still give out those bells when
someone retires. And people still

recite what Rowan said: 'A little Christmas magic keeps out the wrong kind of mischief.'"

"So what does it mean?"

"I have no idea."

Ivar started the engine, and they both sat in silence, lost in thought. Suddenly, a flash of red caught her eye as a cardinal landed on the hood of the truck. In its beak, it carried two small pine twigs naturally grown together in the shape of a heart, with a single red berry nestled where they joined.

The bird placed it gently on the windshield, then flew off into the trees.

Ivar reached out and picked up the sprig, handing it to Holly. "Any idea what this means?"

She shook her head, studying the delicate shape. The more they discovered, the bigger the mystery grew.

TINSEL AND TENSION

<u>Ivar</u>

Holly had barely spoken a word since they'd left the Hale property.

Ivar didn't push. He kept his eyes on the winding road, glancing over occasionally to make sure she was still with him—physically, at least. Emotionally, she looked miles away.

There were things he wanted to tell her, like the way the forest had seemed to pulse as they'd left. He'd heard the slow stretch of sap moving through frozen trunks, a mouse chewing on paper somewhere under the eaves, and what he could have sworn was a fox snoring. He'd always been at-tuned to the woods, but this was different. Sharper. Had the Yule Tree altered him in some way, or was it simply that the experience had made him more attuned to the world around him? And if he could sense these things, could Holly?

And then there was Chad. Ivar could still sense the man's fear of the forest.

But that could wait. Right now, Holly needed him.

By the time they reached his cab-in, dusk had painted the sky in pinks and icy blues. The first stars blinked through the treetops as he parked, climbed out, and came around to open her door. "You need dinner," he said simply.

She followed him inside without a word.

Al trotted over to greet them, tail wagging, nails clicking on the wood floor. He looked from Holly to Ivar and back again, ears pricked as if reading the room. Ivar gestured to him, then Al padded over to Holly, settling beside her on the couch—close enough to comfort, watchful enough to protect. Ivar would thank him with an extra treat at dinner.

The smell of roasting root vegetables and garlic filled the air as Ivar moved around the kitchen. He chopped quietly, giving her space. Holly remained on the couch, arms wrapped around her middle, staring at the crackling fire.

"Ivar," she said finally. "Do you believe in fate?"

He glanced up. "I believe some things are too weird to be coincidences."

She nodded; seconds passed before she spoke again. "Betty Hale knew. About the land. About us. About magic." Her voice caught. "I should have known."

"How?"

She pulled out her phone. "Let's find out."

He watched as she dialed. "Calling your assistant?"

"No," she said. "My father."

The line clicked, and Adam Kringle's voice came through loud enough for him to hear. "Sweetheart! Any news to report?"

"Dad." Holly's tone was sharp. "Did you know about the Hales? That they had a connection to us?"

A pause. "What?"

"I need the truth. No riddles. No side comments about sleigh bells and destiny. The house on the Hale property was full of stuff from our villages. You should have told me."

A sigh. "Holly. If I'd known, I would have told you. But we lost a lot of records in the Eastern Archives fire in the 1970s. A result of too much polyester, I'm afraid. Boxes full of records were lost. We pieced together what we could, but some records were lost forever."

"And you didn't think to mention that when you sent me here?"

"Why would I mention it? I had no idea. I simply sent you to scout a potential workshop site," he said gently. "That's all."

She pressed her lips together, exasperated.

From across the room, Ivar whispered, unable to stop himself, "So... is that really...?"

She nodded. "I'm putting you on speakerphone. Ivar Nilsen's here, and Dad, he's connected to all this somehow."

The voice boomed. "So this is your park ranger. Binoculars, right?"

Ivar froze, a ladle in one hand. He pointed at Holly. "You told him?" he mouthed.

She shook her head. "Dad," Holly said tightly, rubbing her forehead. "This isn't helping. I need answers."

"I understand," Adam replied. "Have you tried contacting Henry?"

"Henry. Of course," she sighed.

"He's been knee-deep in research since the moment he learned of the Yule Tree. Let him know what you need. And Holly, just remember, we don't choose where the magic leads us. We choose whether to follow it."

She rolled her eyes. "Got one in there, huh? Love you. Bye."

The room fell silent. Ivar realized he was still standing there like a statue, the ladle hovering midair.

Holly waved a hand in front of his face. "Sorry about my dad."

Ivar blinked. "Sorry? For what? Santa spoke to me."

"Okay. That's rude. He hasn't delivered toys in years. I'm a Santa too, remember? I don't see you going all loopy when I talk to you."

"Well, yes, but... I mean, no, but... I mean, you're Holly. You don't talk like—"

"Like what? Like this?" Her voice transformed into a perfect imitation. "Ho, ho, ho, Merry Christmas,

Ivar. I hope you've been good this year."

He dropped the ladle.

"Is that what you mean?"

"Yes," he said, voice calm, but his ears turned red. "And I might have just peed myself a little. Please don't ever do that again."

Holly laughed, picking up the ladle and handing it to him, but not before using it to gently whack him on the shoulder. "I won't if you change your sexist attitude."

"Consider it changed," he said, gesturing towards the kitchen. He followed her in, liking the way her presence filled the space. His cabin had always been his retreat. Tonight, with her, it felt like home.

He ached to tell her that. To tell her how much she meant to him. To tell her that some part of him had known her long before today. Before the forest. Before the Yule Tree. But how did a man say that to a woman who'd just talked to Santa on speakerphone? Who was a Santa herself?

So instead he said, "I made roasted squash while Sa—I mean your father was on the line."

"Thank you," she said, then turned to him apologetically. "Pretty weird day, huh?"

He looked at her for a long moment. Then shrugged. "Honestly? Not even the weirdest one this week."

Holly

Holly was tucked under the inn's quilt. She should've been asleep hours ago, but her mind kept replaying the night—the firelight, Ivar's crooked grin, the way he'd said "we" without hesitation. She liked being part of a "we" and an "us." The world didn't feel quite so lonely.

Her phone buzzed.

Ivar: Is this the North Pole?
Holly: Be careful. You're on
    the "nice but leaning towards
    naughty" list.
Ivar: That tracks. I think you might
    be on the "works too hard and
    forgets to have fun" list.
Holly: Ouch. Accurate.
Ivar: You did laugh tonight, though.
    Twice, I think? That's progress.
Holly: If you count laughing at you
    dropping a ladle.
Ivar: I'll take it. Night, Kringle.
Holly: Night, Ranger.

She set the phone down, but the glow still painted her ceiling in soft light. Her body was tired, but her heart—her heart was awake.

It had been years since someone had made her laugh like this. Years since she'd let someone see her this unguarded.

And she wasn't sure what scared her more: that she wanted to see him again tomorrow, or that she already knew she would.

18
days until
Christmas Eve

BREAKING THE ICE

<u>Ivar</u>

Ivar poured himself a coffee while Al was sprawled in front of the stove, paws twitching in a dream. Picking up his phone, his thumb hovered over last night's messages.

For someone who claimed to hate surprises, Holly Kringle had sure become one he liked very, very much. In one short, but incredibly full week, she'd turned his world upside down, inside out, and given it quite a good shake.

And now it was the first day of the Christmas Carnival and the kick-off to Operation: Christmas Arc the Hales.

He wondered if she was awake yet and if she, too, had spent the night replaying everything between them. He thumbed open their chat and started typing.

Ivar: Woke up to find roasted squash in the fridge and lingering trauma from hearing you say "ho ho ho." Thanks for that.
Holly: Consider it an early Christmas gift.
Ivar: Pretty sure that's what nightmares are made of.
Holly: Then you're welcome.
Ivar: You bringing your broom today or should I clear the skies first?
Holly: Keep it up, Ranger, and I'll turn you into coal.

Ivar: Worth it.

Ivar stared at the screen for a while before setting the phone down beside his coffee. Outside, the trees were dusted in light snow, the world still and waiting. He had no idea where any of this was going, only that it had a momentum of its own and he would follow it wherever it led.

Holly

Holly arrived at the carnival just as the church bells rang noon. The town square had been transformed with strings of lights draped from lamppost to lamppost, and garland wound around every post.

"I've never seen it look so good," one woman said, making Holly smile. She may have popped by on her broom last night and given it a little Santa zhuzhing.

She scanned the crowd, searching for Ivar. Children darted past with candy canes and Santa hats, the air alive with laughter and the squeak of snow boots. On the main stage, the mayor stood proudly beside Rowan and Chad Hale, both in matching red sashes that read CARNIVAL GRAND MARSHAL in glittering gold letters.

Liv had outdone herself.

She sensed him before she saw him, as if he were a planet coming into her orbit.

"Sorry, I'm late," Ivar said, brushing past her, snowflakes melting in his hair. "These two—" he nodded toward Liv's boys, "said they'd be ready in five minutes, but their version of five minutes is twenty in real time."

Wyatt grinned, tugging his hat lower. "Hey, I couldn't find my favorite sweater. We're gonna get hot chocolate, okay, Uncle Ivar? Mom gave us money."

"Sure," Ivar said. "Meet me back here in an hour."

"Okay!" The boys took off through the crowd, laughter trailing behind them.

Holly smirked. "He likes a girl."

Ivar blinked. "What?"

"Wyatt. That's why he needed the sweater." She gestured toward the cocoa stand, where two girls about Wyatt's age were giggling behind paper cups, their cheeks pink from the cold.

"Oh," Ivar said, realization dawning. "I didn't know Santa knew that kind of thing, too."

"It's not magic, Ivar. It's observation. Sometimes you just need to pay attention," Holly said with a small smile.

"Like with my binoculars."

"Exactly."

"Except that your father…"

She shrugged and linked her arm through his. "Sometimes it is magic."

The mayor stepped up to the microphone, tapping it once until the feedback squealed across the square. "Welcome, everyone, to Winterwood's Annual Christmas Carnival!"

The crowd cheered.

Holly leaned toward Ivar. "He sounds like he's been practicing in the mirror all week."

"Probably has," Ivar murmured.

The mayor continued, voice booming: "This year, we are especially honored to have as our Grand Marshals the new stewards of the Hale property—Rowan and Chad Hale!"

Polite applause rippled through the crowd. Rowan beamed, waving to the audience. Chad, on the other hand, looked as comfortable as a man enduring a dentist appointment for a reality TV show. His smile was tight, his eyes already scanning for an escape route.

Holly's heart tightened. The tension was almost tangible, and the cheer of the crowd balanced on the edge of politeness, not warmth. The plan had begun, but this wasn't how she'd pictured it.

Everyone was polite, but not welcoming.

We need joy, she thought. Belonging. Fun.

Without thinking, she reached for Ivar's hand. His fingers curled instinctively around hers. Then she didn't think, didn't try; she simply wished.

The air seemed to hush and soften. The lights strung along the eaves flickered once before glowing brighter. A child's laughter rang out, bright and clear as sleigh bells. And then, from somewhere near the cocoa stand, came the sharp whump of a snowball hitting its mark.

Another followed. Then another. Within seconds, the whole square erupted into a good-natured snowball fight. Laughter and shouts rose above the town like music, mittens were flying, and people were ducking behind snowbanks and benches.

Holly laughed, startled by the sudden wave of joy. Ivar's hand was still in hers, his expression half wonder, half awe.

"Did you...?" he began.

"I don't know," she said softly. "I think I did, but I'm not sure. I usually use my magic for more practical things."

"Like Santas in my latte foam and toy deliveries?"

"Exactly," she said, grinning, but inside, this felt significant. Like she'd remembered how to breathe.

The snowball flurry lasted only a few minutes, but it was enough to shift everything. The stiffness in the air melted into laughter; strangers smiled at one another,

Rowan was laughing with the mayor, and even Chad had a smile on his face as he brushed snow from his coat.

When the mayor finally stepped back to the microphone, his hat askew and cheeks flushed, the crowd quieted on cue, still grinning. "Well," he said, chuckling, "I can see Winterwood's enthusiasm hasn't cooled any this year. And now, before we all freeze solid, let's officially begin our festivities with Chad and Rowan Hale judging our ice-carving contest."

Applause rippled through the square, louder and lighter now, carried by true excitement instead of courtesy. Holly squeezed Ivar's hand one last time before letting go.

"That," she whispered, "was phase one."

He smiled. "I'd call it a success."

Holly stayed near Ivar at first, caught by the echo of magic. Then, remembering the plan, she nodded toward the judges' stand. "I'll keep an eye on Rowan."

"So that leaves me with Chad," he said, adjusting his hat with a wry smile.

"Exactly," she teased, and moved through the crowd.

Rowan stood beside the carvers, cider in hand, watching a group of teenagers attempt a bear that looked halfway to becoming a moose. They waved her over, laughing, and she gamely joined them, accepting a tiny ice cup one of the kids had carved and toasting them with mock ceremony. The sound of her laughter lifted something in Holly's chest.

Across the square, Chad lingered at the edge of the crowd, posture stiff but eyes tracking the carvers. Emma passed by with a tray of cookie samples, her hair tumbling out from beneath her red hat. When she offered him one, he startled slightly, then accepted with a tentative smile. She said something Holly couldn't hear, and he actually laughed.

Holly smiled to herself. Phase one, indeed.

She joined Rowan, handing her a napkin with a warm cinnamon bun from Emma's stall. "You looked like you were having fun."

Rowan grinned. "I forgot how nice this could be. I like Seattle, but nothing beats a small-town festival."

They watched in companionable silence for a moment. Then Rowan's voice lowered. "I'm sorry if Chad was at the cabin. I mean, weirder than usual."

Holly followed her gaze. Chad had moved closer to Emma's booth, both of them laughing now.

"He told me once the place always gave him the creeps," Rowan said quietly. "He said it made him feel watched. I think he's afraid to go back."

"Afraid?" Holly echoed.

"Not of ghosts. Just... something he doesn't understand. And Chad doesn't like not understanding things." Rowan gave a small, sad smile. "We were never close growing up, and now we're almost strangers. Once our parents died, we were sent to different schools on different coasts. He's also seven years older than me, so we never spent summers together. This project was supposed to fix that. First, he convinced me to sell so we could invest in something togeth-er. Then he had the resort idea. I never wanted to sell, and I certain-ly don't want to touch the forest, but I want a relationship with my brother. I guess I thought being in Winterwood together would help."

"Then we'll make sure it does."

Rowan's smile warmed. "You sound like my aunt Betty."

"Smart woman," Holly said, and they both laughed softly, the sound mingling with the rhythmic chip of chisels.

ICY WHAT YOU DID THERE

<u>Holly</u>

With the ice-carving contest wrapping up, Holly looped her arm through Ivar's as they collected his nephews and began the walk back toward the inn. The boys ran ahead, bounding through the snow on a sugar high, their laughter echoing down the street, reminding her of that easy kind of happiness she'd shared with her siblings.

Around them, the crowd had thinned to clusters of families lingering near the cocoa stand.

Laughter still drifted through the air, and the occasional comment about the snowball fight left her smiling.

Then, a flash of red snagged her attention.

A little girl, no more than six, came rushing through the crowd, a potted poinsettia clutched awkwardly in her mittened hands. The pot was too large for her small arms, and as she hurried past, her boot caught on an uneven patch of snow. The slip was so quick it made Holly gasp.

The girl tumbled forward with a startled cry. The poinsettia flew from her grasp, hitting the ground with a dull crack. The main stem snapped clean through, the vibrant red leaves scattered across the snow.

"My flower!" the girl wailed, tears immediately welling in her eyes. "It's broken! I bought it for Grandma with my own money!"

Holly's instinct was to reach for the girl, but Ivar was already there, crouching down to her level.

"Hey, it's okay," he said gently. "Let's take a look."

Holly watched as he gathered the fallen plant, his hands steady and careful as he nestled the broken stem back into the pot. What happened next made her breath catch.

As Ivar's fingers brushed the broken stem, a subtle shimmer—like heat rising from summer pavement—rippled across the plant. The stem straightened, its severed edges knitting together seamlessly. The scattered leaves perked up, their color deepening from pale to vibrant red.

The girl's tears stopped abruptly. "You fixed it!" she exclaimed, taking the pot from him with reverent care.

"There you go," Ivar said with a warm smile. "It just needed to be put back in its soil. Plants are tougher than they look."

The child beamed, hugging the pot to her chest before scampering off toward an elderly woman waiting by the raffle booth.

Holly stared at him, her mind racing. "How did you do that?" she asked quietly.

Ivar turned, brow furrowed. "Do what?"

"Fix that plant."

"I didn't fix it," he said, brushing soil from his palms. "I repotted it."

"Ivar," Holly said carefully, "the stem was completely broken. Snapped in half."

He looked genuinely confused. "No, it wasn't. It just lost a couple of leaves. The stem was bent, not broken."

Holly studied his face, searching for any sign that he was aware of what had happened. There was nothing but calm confusion.

A chill that had nothing to do with the winter air ran through her. She'd been so focused on the Hales that she hadn't fully considered what was happening with Ivar. The tree. The cardinals. And now this.

While that experience under the tree had changed them both—how could it not?—something in him had changed. He had changed. There was a confidence, a contentedness, that was almost contagious when he was near. And that light in his eyes that drew her in... she should have paid more attention since that day in the forest.

She'd never been one to study magic, never curious about its origins. She used it when it was needed, never questioning where it came from. But Ivar hadn't been born into it. He'd gone into the forest as an ordinary man and walked out with an ancient magic flowing through him.

She didn't press Ivar further, not wanting to alarm him. Instead, she pulled out her phone and typed a quick message to her brother.

Holly: Call me tonight. Urgent.

By the time they reached the inn, daylight had faded behind the ridge, leaving the snow-covered world washed in lavender and silver. The boys waved as they ran back to their house while Holly and Ivar stepped inside.

Liv looked up from refilling a tray of cookies. "There you are! I was starting to wonder if you two had snuck off to join the carvers."

"Tempting," Ivar said, pulling off his gloves. "But I value my fingers too much."

"Speak for yourself," Holly added. "Some of those carvers had serious skill. There was a dragon. A slightly lopsided dragon, but still."

"I saw that taking shape before I had to come back here." Liv grinned and motioned them toward a table near the fire. "Hot cocoa's on the house tonight. You both earned it. And I want a full report."

Holly sat, grateful for the warmth that sank into her bones. "It went well. Rowan was lovely. She talked to all the carvers, took pictures with the kids, and helped hand out cookies. She admitted that the reason she's supporting Chad on this project is to grow close to him again."

"Oh," Liv said, placing a hand over her heart. "That is so sweet. I just wish they could find a project to work on that didn't destroy the forest. And what about Chad?"

"Ask Emma," Ivar said.

"Emma?"

"There was flirting."

"I'll definitely ask her then," Liv said, pouring steaming cocoa into mugs. "So maybe your plan will work."

Holly smiled into her cup. "For what it's worth, Rowan genuinely likes it here. You can see it in her eyes."

Liv's smile softened. "Then she's the key to reaching Chad."

The room quieted, the only sounds being the pop of the fire and the clink of mugs. Holly's gaze drifted to the window, where a paper snowflake hung, turning slowly in the warm air. For a moment, she imagined the roots of the Yule Tree stretching beneath the earth in a luminous web, as intricate and singular as that snowflake. She could almost feel its pulse. Not inside her, but between them. She remembered the subtle shift in the air when she and Ivar joined hands at the carnival, and the snowball fight ensued. That hadn't been typical Santa magic. It had been something else. Something shared? Because Ivar had magic of his own?

"Anyway," Liv said, breaking the silence, "the next event we have them in is the Tree Hunt. If we can convince the Hales to join in—not just to judge—that might seal it. Show them the heart of this town."

Holly nodded. "What exactly happens at a tree hunt?"

Liv brightened. "Oh, it's the best tradition. Everyone pairs up in teams and searches the forest for the perfect Christmas tree. There's snacks, sleigh bells, friendly competition. The mayor gives out a trophy for 'Best Tree,' but mostly it's just fun."

Ivar leaned closer, his shoulder brushing hers as he lowered his voice. "We're definitely winning that trophy."

"Oh really? Confident much?" she teased.

"I'm the ranger," he murmured. "I have a reputation to uphold."

"Ivar," Liv said, "would you mind grabbing the boys? I don't feel like cooking tonight, so they can have dinner here. They're probably stuffed with maple candy and popcorn, but I'd like to get a vegetable or two into them."

"Sure thing," he said, grabbing his coat.

"I could have texted them," Liv said once he was gone, "but I wanted to talk to you."

"What about?"

"What you've done for my brother. I don't know what's going on with you two, but he's changed since you got here. He never joins trivia night, he always avoids the carnival, and he's never participated in the Tree Hunt. Yet he just said you're going to win. He's become a different person. Thank you. He's got a spark I thought I'd never see again."

Holly didn't know what to say. She stared into her mug, watching the tiny ripples fade. "We're a good team," she said softly. "He's helped me too. My entire life has focused on work; he's reminded me how to have fun."

They were a good team. She felt it in every glance that lingered too long, every unspoken thought that seemed to echo between them. But now she wondered if what bound them was truly theirs or if the magic itself had drawn them together.

Liv smiled, lifting her mug. "Well, I think you've given him a little Christmas spirit, and I'm glad for it. To new friends and whatever comes next."

Holly clinked her cup to Liv's, the smile lingering on her lips even as unease began to stir. Whatever comes next was starting to worry her.

ARE YULE SERIOUS?

Holly

Holly's phone rang the second she stepped into her room. Henry!

"Tell me you found something."

"Hello to you too," Henry said. "And yes. I've been digging through the archives since Dad called. And then doubled down after your message. You're not going to believe what I found."

"What?"

"I'm sending you a photo right now."

It was a scanned parchment with singed edges and faded ink. Holly sat on the edge of the bed, tapping to enlarge it. Symbols she half-recognized wound around a central illustration: a great tree with radiating roots, each curling outward like rivers of light.

"Okay," Henry continued. "Most of this comes from what survived the 1700s records—the pre-Santa era, when the North Network was still forming. I found references to a "Heart Tree," or sometimes "the Root of Light." According to the notes, every magical current—the veins that feed our workshops, sleigh routes, even the auroras—originates from one central source."

Holly frowned, tracing the faint lines of script. "The Yule Tree," she murmured. "But Henry, we already know this legend."

"Patience, Hol. I'm getting there. I'm piecing this together bit by bit from different texts, some of which require translating. But if I'm correct, the Yule Tree isn't just a source of power." He took a deep breath. "It's alive in a way we don't really understand. The notes say the Yule Tree chooses when to reveal itself. It calls out to those it trusts to protect it. They're called Guardians."

She stilled, remembering the whisper in the shower.

"Every record of the tree's reappearance coincides with a moment of imbalance. When the world drifts too far toward disconnection, the Guardian is called. And get this—the Guardian isn't a Kringle. They're someone of the land. Someone rooted there, and tied to the magic instinctively."

Ivar.

Her mouth went so dry she couldn't speak.

"There's more," Henry continued, "but I'm still piecing things togeth-er. However, I can tell you that if the Yule Tree is ever destroyed, the lines fracture, the North weak-ens, and the auroras fade."

Holly sank back against the head-board, phone still pressed to her ear. Outside, the wind sighed against the window, stirring the snow.

"Henry." Her voice was barely au-dible. "Ivar, the forest ranger, saw the tree too."

There was a long pause be-fore Henry spoke. "That could

only mean one thing. Ivar is the Guardian."

This time it was her turn to pause as she collected her thoughts. "He saw it as a child, like the legend says." She imagined her brother frantically taking notes. "I have one more question. Is there any mention of powers bestowed upon the Guardian?"

"Powers? Nothing specific that I've come across, but I think it's safe to infer that the Guardian must have some kind of ability if they are to protect the Yule Tree. Why? What has the Guardian done?"

The Guardian. "I saw Ivar heal a plant. The stem was broken and then healed by Ivar's touch."

"Are you sure?"

"Henry, yes. Of course I'm sure." Her voice rose with impatience. "Please keep digging."

"I will, but I've pretty much gone through our entire archives."

"I know you're doing your best. But Ivar and I are stumbling around in the dark." She stood, moved to the window, and somehow knocked over the broomstick.

Of course.

"Have you contacted the Befana side of the family?" she asked.

"No, why?"

"I might not have told Dad everything." She explained about the broom and La Befana's words.

"You should have mentioned this before," Henry said, using his older-brother-knows-better tone.

"I have a lot going on. And then there's the Hales. How are they connected?"

"And don't forget about Christmas. It's only two weeks away."

"Helpful, thanks. It's not like I haven't been keeping track. Those daily alerts from Dad's office wouldn't let me forget if I tried."

"Hang in there, Hol. I'll do my best."

Holly set her phone on the nightstand and stared at the ceiling, one word filling the room as if it were a ghost. Guardian.

She reached for her broom. "Did you know this?" Of course, it remained still. "You're supposed to be guiding me... so guide. How do I tell Ivar he's a Guardian?" Snow drifted lazily past the window, catching the light of the streetlamps. Beyond them, the forest lay still and dark, a sleeping giant beneath the stars.

The thought of Ivar out there—his steady presence, his quiet reverence for every tree, every ripple of wind—sent a pang through her chest. Of course the magic would choose him.

Her phone buzzed. A new message from Ivar. She smiled despite her worries.

Ivar: You awake, Kringle?
Holly: Maybe. Why?
Ivar: I'm prepping for the Tree Hunt. You bringing your broom?
Holly: Only if I can use it to knock you off your sled.
Ivar: See, that's the Christmas spirit. Get some sleep. You'll need it.
Holly: You too, Ranger.

She set the phone down again, her smile fading into thought.

Tomorrow, they'd search for the Winterwood Christmas tree. And she'd have to decide if she was

ready to tell him the truth—that
the tree he'd been searching for all
his life might have been searching
for him too.

17
days until
Christmas Eve

TREE-MENDOUS FUN

Ivar

The annual Winterwood Tree Hunt was one of those events the whole town turned out for. Except Ivar. He'd always found an excuse to skip it, though he didn't mind helping later when it came time to haul the chosen tree back to the square. Participating, though? That had never been his thing.

But this year was different. Having Holly by his side changed that.

From their spot in the crowd, he watched Emma climb onto a pickup bed, clipboard in hand, her red hat bobbing like a cherry against the gray sky. "All right, folks!" she called from above the crowd, her voice carrying easily over the chatter. "This year, we're shaking things up. No more same-old teams. You'll be paired at random!"

A chorus of groans rolled through the crowd, followed by laughter.

"That's right," Emma went on. "It's time to make new friends—or new enemies, depending on who steals the saw."

Beside him, Tess elbowed his arm. "You just don't want to get paired with me. I cut trees like they owe me money."

"Remind me not to run up my bar tab," Eli said dryly from behind her.

Tess grinned. "You got that right."

Names were drawn from Emma's basket, with each pair met with cheers or mock groans. "Eli Brennan and Tess Callahan!" Emma read. "Try not to burn down the forest, you two."

"Can't make promises!" Tess called back.

Next came "Marty Callahan and George Keating!"

George tipped his cap. "I'll keep him from writing poetry about the tree, don't worry."

Laughter rippled through the crowd, but when Emma's grin turned mischievous, Ivar's stomach sank.

"Next up..." she said, milking the moment, "Ivar Nilsen and—" she paused, her voice full of mischief—"Chad Hale!"

Ivar and Chad exchanged polite smiles.

"I thought Rowan and I were judges," Chad said.

"Like I said," Emma replied, "we're changing things up this year. Holly Kringle and Rowan Hale are judges."

Ivar gently nudged Holly. "Judge now, eh?"

"I'll have you know that this is far from my first Christmas tree judging contest, so I'm bringing a wealth of knowledge and experience to this event."

They both laughed, but he'd noticed something missing from their banter today, like she was distracted. She'd opened up so much in the last few days, laughing more, trading playful texts, but today she seemed quieter. Granted, the protection of the Yule Tree was important, but he could feel her stress, and there was something else.

Holly tapped his arm, then pointed to Chad.

He muttered something under his breath to Rowan. The man was not happy about this, but to his credit, he was willing to go along with it.

Emma clapped her hands. "All right, everyone. Teams ready? Remember, we're looking for the town tree. We need something tall, symmetrical, and full of Christmas spirit. And no cutting yet! Just mark your finds with the red ribbon."

"Good luck, Ranger," Holly said, reaching up and placing a kiss on his cheek. The brush of her lips against his skin sent a ripple through him, like sunlight spreading across frozen water. The warmth she left behind burned faintly, as though her magic had marked him.

"You have 15 minutes, starting... now!"

Ivar joined Chad and directed him into the forest. They were on the outskirts of town, so it was quiet, with just the hush of wind through pine needles, and the faint creak of the snow underfoot. To Ivar, it was heaven on earth. Chad clearly didn't share that opinion. Though he kept a measured pace, his posture was stiff, like he was so tightly wound, the slightest thing would set him off.

"You do this every year?" Chad asked, breathing hard.

"The town does, yes," Ivar said. "I usually help with the cutting and the transportation."

"So they paired me with a rookie?"

"I am the park ranger, so I do know my way around the forest."

They trudged deeper. The air had that crisp, resinous smell that made Ivar's lungs ache in the best way. He took a deep breath, feeling grounded, happy, home.

Chad grew even quieter.

"You don't like the forest much, do you?" Ivar asked.

"No, not really. I prefer the city. It's alive and energetic."

"Most people think the forest is still. It's not. It's alive. You just have to listen."

"Alive?" Chad sounded almost panicked. "You mean the trees and animals, right?"

"Well, of course it's alive. Otherwise, the trees would be dead, but what I mean is..." He paused. What did he mean? "You have to think about the entire ecosystem. Everything has its role, and everything works together. It's not about trees, or plants, or animals. It's what they create together, the forest as a whole."

"You're pretty philosophical for a park ranger."

"Apparently I am."

Chad walked ahead, Ivar following in his footsteps. He started feeling a bit off. With each step, the air grew heavier, the light dimmer. The forest blurred, reshaping itself. A boy ran ahead of him now. He was bundled in a blue coat, his laughter sharp against the cold air. Snow sprayed beneath his boots as he ran, oblivious of the ledge ahead. If he didn't stop, he'd run right off the edge. "Look out," Ivar yelled as loud as he could. The boy turned, fear in his eyes.

Ivar stopped short, heart pounding. The image flickered, dissolving into mist. The boy was gone. Only Chad stood there, staring at him.

With the same eyes.

A realization tugged at the edge of Ivar's mind, and while it was too strange to believe, he couldn't dismiss it. He'd just seen a memory.

"You okay?" Chad asked.

"Yeah. Fine. Let's look around here."

Chad went to the left, Ivar to the right. With Chad out of sight, he ducked behind a tree. The image of the boy still lingered. What was going on?

He bent forward, hands on knees, drawing deep breaths until the world steadied again. Focus. He thought of his cabin by the pond, Al curled up by the fire, and the steady rhythm of the woods. He thought of Holly, her laughter, her courage, the way she looked when light caught her hair.

And then, unbidden, came the thought of a tree. The perfect tree for a Kringle. For Holly. It was tall, balanced, and aglow with life. A Christmas tree worthy of her.

When he opened his eyes, the forest felt different. Brighter somehow, even though the sun had set.

"Ivar," Chad called. He was close. In fact, he was on the other side of the tree Ivar had ducked behind. "Check it out. I think I found the tree."

He turned slowly. There, right beside him, stood a spruce unlike the rest. Perfectly shaped, its branches dusted in snow that seemed to shimmer faintly.

He walked around the tree, standing beside Chad.

"It's perfect," Chad said. "I've never seen anything like it."

"Me neither." Except he had. Only seconds ago, in his mind.

They both knew this would be the winning tree.

Ivar pulled a length of red ribbon from his pocket and tied it to the tree's lowest branch, just as the timing whistle sounded signaling the end of the contest.

For a brief moment, Ivar thought he saw a faint glow pulse through the bark—subtle, like the embers of a campfire. When he blinked, it was gone.

The teams were laughing and enjoying cookies courtesy of the Maple Mug while they waited for the judging.

When Holly spotted Ivar, her eyes lit up, making Ivar's heart thud loudly. The memory of that kiss warmed his cheek all over again.

"We've made our decision," she told him.

"I know we won," he leaned in and whispered. "Thanks to you. Another bit of Santa magic?"

She didn't reply. She didn't have to. Her face said it all.

"You didn't...?" he asked.

She shook her head. "No. Wasn't me."

"But it's so perfect. Too perfect." He turned toward her fully now, searching for answers.

Holly reached out and took his hands.

Before he could speak, Liv and Rowan appeared, cheeks flushed, laughing and glowing from either too much cider or George's special hot chocolate. Liv looped her arm through Holly's with a grin. "I'm stealing your girl, Ivar. We've got a date with the hot tub."

Holly squeezed his hands once more, her eyes steady. "Trust me," she mouthed before being swept into the crowd.

Snow lifted in her wake, swirling in a small spiral that danced around his boots before settling again.

Ivar stood still, his palms tingling where she'd touched him. Beneath the snow, the hum deepened. It was no longer a mystery, but a question.

To which his heart answered: Yes. He absolutely trusted her.

The tree looked even bigger strapped to the flatbed than it had standing proudly in the clearing.

"This is going to be a pain to unload," Chad muttered, arms crossed, surveying the majestic pine.

Ivar smirked. Chad, despite his complaining, was more relaxed than Ivar had ever seen him. Their plan was working. They'd managed somehow to crack his carefully built cynicism. "I didn't hear you complaining when you won."

"I didn't realize I'd signed up for... this." Chad waved his arms at the back of the truck. "Where's your sister anyway? Isn't she in charge of this festival?"

"She and Holly took Rowan to soak in the inn's hot tub. You, however, have been volunteered."

Chad muttered something under his breath that Ivar chose not to decode.

They'd barely backed the truck into the designated spot when a crew of townsfolk descended—cheerful, mittened, full of brewery-fueled enthusiasm.

"Here comes our hero!" Emma declared.

Chad blinked. "Is she talking about me?"

"Yeah." Ivar handed him a pair of gloves. "Try to enjoy it. You earned this weird parade."

As the tree was carefully raised into place, with strings of lights and cheerful commentary, Chad didn't retreat. He didn't grimace much and even laughed when a kid asked if the star should be 'eco-certified.'

And Ivar noticed the way Chad smiled more around the town's Maple Mug proprietor.

"You good?" Ivar asked once the tree stood tall, glowing from a thousand lights.

Chad hesitated, hands in his coat pockets. "It wasn't the worst day I've ever had. This last bit was surprisingly fun. What is it about this place?"

"Winterwood will have that effect on you," Ivar said. "Now, to the Sugarhouse." He noted the confusion on Chad's face. "It's a brewery."

"Now that's more like it," Chad said.

The warm lights of the brewery spilled across the snow. Inside, Tess and Marty had cleared space for the ad hoc tree crew, and someone shoved a craft brew into Chad's hand before he could protest.

"To Chad," someone toasted. "Savior of the town's Christmas aesthetic!"

Chad shook his head, amused. "That's a stretch."

Ivar clinked his glass against Chad's. "It's the best tree we've had in years. Take the win."

They slid into a booth, the scent of pine sap clinging to their jackets. Ivar watched Chad take it all in—Emma laughing in the corner, Marty handing out samples of a new mulled beer blend, Eli, a born storyteller, sharing tales around the fire.

For the first time, he saw it reach him.

This wasn't just a town. It was a home. A place that made space for people. Even unlikely ones. People like Chad.

People like him.

SPA-LA-LA-LA-LA

<u>Holly</u>

Holly sank deeper into the hot tub, listening to the laughter from the Sugarhouse that drifted up through the cold. She was wondering if Ivar was there yet when her phone buzzed on the side table. A knowing smile tugged at her lips before she even picked it up.

Ivar: No casualties setting up the tree. Chad even carried the saw.
Holly: So we're calling that progress?

Ivar: Definite Christmas miracle. Our team is basking in the praise.
Holly: Tempted to leave you both there to become small-town legends.
Ivar: Too late. Chad's already halfway to honorary lumberjack.
Holly: [laughing emoji]
Holly: We're drying off soon and will join you. Save me a gingerbread stout?
Ivar: Only if you promise not to enchant it.
Holly: No promises.

A laugh escaped. She couldn't help it.

Across from her, Liv raised an eyebrow. "Texting anyone interesting?"

"Just logistics for tomorrow," Holly said, but the heat in her cheeks gave her away.

"Uh-huh." Liv's grin was far too knowing. "Funny how logistics make you smile like that."

Rowan laughed, tucking a damp strand of hair behind her ear. "Who's the lucky one?"

"Ivar," Holly said, her cheeks turning redder. "We were talking about the tree."

"Oh yes, the legendary spruce," Liv said. "Quite the upset, having your brother win."

Rowan chuckled. "You should've seen his face when Emma announced it. I don't think Chad's ever been so confused about being happy."

"He handled himself well," Liv said, sipping from her mug of cider.

Rowan nodded. "He did. It's nice to see him laugh."

The steam rose around them, softening the world to a haze.

"So," Holly said, "you mentioned you're a professor?"

"Environmental history," Rowan replied. "Land use and conservation. It's not quite thrilling dinner conversation, but I love it. Aunt Betty had a lot to do with that."

"But you're going to develop the land," Holly said. It seemed so contradictory.

Rowan sighed. "I know. It's complicated. Chad and I... we didn't grow up close. This project is our way of reconnecting."

"Tell us about Betty," Liv said. "We all knew her, but not well."

"She was wonderful. A bit eccentric, but in the best way. When I stayed with her, every day felt special. We'd walk in the forest or bake bread."

"I only stopped by her place a couple of times," Liv said. "It always felt like the walls had stories."

"They still do," Rowan said. "The attic too." She laughed. "I found boxes of journals—dozens of them—dating back to the 1800s. I almost fell through the ceiling trying to get them down."

Holly leaned forward. "Journals?"

Rowan nodded. "Old family journals, filled with notes, sketches, and strange little diagrams. I thought Chad might toss them, so I brought them to Mim at the library. She's going to review them to determine if they belong in the town archives."

"Good thinking," Liv said. "Mim guards those archives like a dragon with a hoard."

Rowan grinned. "That's not surprising. She said she'd call me next week and let me know."

Holly swirled the water, though her pulse quickened. Journals from the 1800s. This might be the missing link between the Hales, the Kringles, and Ivar.

"Let me know what she finds," Holly said. "I'd love to see them myself."

"Of course," Rowan said. "Aunt Betty always said our family had deep roots here. Maybe those journals will tell us what she meant."

Liv sighed, stretching her legs. "Well, whatever they say, I'm calling this the perfect end to a perfect Winterwood day."

Holly smiled, but her mind was already miles away. They had to see those journals.

TROUBLE BREWING

<u>Holly</u>

The laughter from the Sugarhouse Brewery still echoed faintly in Holly's mind as she slipped through the quiet halls of the Winterwood Inn.

The townsfolk had filled the brewery with friendship and noise—Tess leading a toast to "the conquering tree hunters," Marty strumming an old guitar near the fire, Rowan laughing until she cried when Chad tried (and failed) to tell a Vermont joke.

And Ivar, beside her at the bar, had leaned in just enough for his shoulder to brush hers. "Looks like your plan's working," he'd murmured, eyes on Rowan and Chad across the room.

She'd smiled. "Maybe. But it's early yet."

Still, she grew hopeful. Rowan was changing. Winterwood had gotten under her skin; it showed in the way she looked at the people, the town, the mountains. Even Chad had seemed lighter. He'd bought a round for the room, for heaven's sake.

Things were looking up.

But Ivar sensed she was keeping something from him. When they'd stepped outside to cool off, he'd studied her face.

"You're quiet," he'd said. "Something wrong?"

She'd shaken her head too quickly. "Just tired."

He'd frowned, not quite believing her, but he hadn't pressed. That was the thing about Ivar—he listened, knowing when to push and when to step back.

Now, in the stillness of her room, the omission (it wasn't quite a lie) itched at her.

Holly picked up her phone and scrolled to Henry's number. He answered on the second ring, sounding half-asleep but instantly alert when she mentioned the journals.

"Rowan found them in Betty Hale's attic," she said. "They're with the librarian for review, but if they date back to the 1800s..."

"What a find," Henry said. "Hang on one second."

She heard him riffling through papers.

"Does a Cornelius Hale sound familiar?"

"No, but they share a last name."

"I think he was a craftsman—one of the old North Village retirees. We lost most of the records in that '70s fire, but I started asking around. A few of the old-timers remember hearing about him. One guy swears his grandfather said Cornelius left the North after retirement. Settled somewhere 'where the light sleeps under the ground.'"

"That has to be Winterwood."

"That's my guess, based on his last name. The craftsmen have a name for those who leave but are drawn to Yule veins. Keepers. As if the power beneath is a comfort, like a second heartbeat. Cornelius Hale was likely drawn there because of the vein. Whether he or his descendants knew about the Yule Tree is anyone's guess, but this might be the missing link."

"Could he have been a Guardian?"

"I don't think so. He wasn't from there, and then there's his age. But I mean, anything's possible. This whole Guardian thing is new to all of us. But my educated guess is that he was a Keeper."

Holly's brow furrowed. "So, Cornelius Hale—"

"Settled in Winterwood because of the pull. My guess is he never knew the Yule Tree was there. But over time, it might have come to him in dreams or visions. And if it did, he realized he wasn't meant to use the land, but to protect it. That's why his property was never developed for generations. Of course, it might be nothing more than luck or coincidence."

Holly pressed a hand to her temple.

"I'll see if I can take a look at the journals tomorrow," she said quietly.

"Good plan," Henry replied. "And, Hol?"

"Yeah?"

"If those journals are relevant and you brought them here, you'd never have to get me a Christmas present ever again."

Holly laughed. "I'll do my best."

The call ended, leaving her in silence. There was still so much to learn. And while they were all scrambling to do that, Ivar—steady, kind, impossibly grounded Ivar—had no idea the Yule Tree had chosen him as Guardian.

Holly closed her eyes and whispered, "How am I supposed to tell him?"

She hated not knowing. The helplessness scraped at her. You couldn't make decisions without facts, so fine, they'd get some. This was a project that needed managing, and she would manage it. She might not understand magical trees or Guardians, but if Holly Kringle knew how to do anything, it was how to take charge.

She grabbed a notebook and made a list. Short, but concrete. Action. Direction. It steadied her pulse. Then she reached for her phone to text Ivar, only to find fifty unread emails and two unopened messages from Rita.

Normally, that sight would have made her twitch. Red notification bubbles gave her a physical ache. Tonight, though, none of that mattered.

The team at NED could handle things. They were good—she'd trained them well.

What mattered now was solving this mystery, saving the Yule Tree, and helping Ivar. She ignored the noise and opened the one thread that mattered.

Holly: Busy tomorrow morning, Ranger?
Ivar: Depends. Is this about forest permits or another top-secret Kringle broom operation?
Holly: Neither. It's a high-stakes research mission.
Ivar: Dangerous. Do I need my snowshoes or my bear spray?

Holly: Library card. A travel mug is optional.

Ivar: ...A library date?

Holly: Of sorts. We're investigating 19th-century journals and possible supernatural land stewards.

Ivar: Sounds romantic.

Holly: You have a very broad definition of romance.

Ivar: You're the one inviting me to spend a morning surrounded by dusty books and local gossip.

Holly: Promise me you won't flirt with the librarian.

Ivar: No promises. Mim's been trying to recruit me for trivia night ever since our big win.

Holly: Figures. Be there at ten.

Ivar: Should I bring coffee?

Holly: Only if it comes with sarcasm and patience.

Ivar: I never leave home without them.

16
days until
Christmas Eve

READ BETWEEN THE PINES

<u>Holly</u>

Mim Daley peered at Holly over a stack of books, her glasses perched halfway down her nose. Her cardigan, purple with a sequined snowflake brooch, looked like it had been chosen for maximum whimsy. A black cat lounged across the checkout counter.

"Ah, Miss Kringle. I was so excited when you called this morning about the journals. We can set you up in the reading alcove where it's warmest. I figured you'd like a little privacy."

Ivar stepped inside, brushing snow from his shoulders. His hair was damp from melting flakes, and a blush of cold colored his cheeks.

Mim's smile widened. "Well, if it isn't our Forest Philosopher. Don't tell me you've come to finally return those field guides?"

Ivar gave her a mock salute. "Eventually."

Mim's laugh was bright and delightful. "You're just lucky you're handsome enough to get away with overdue fees. Now, tell me, Miss Kringle—"

"Holly, please."

"Yes, Holly. Tell me, are you related to the Hales, dear?"

"No," Holly said. "I'm a bit of a local history buff."

"Wonderful," Mim said. "Now, Ivar, come with me. They're still in the back. Holly dear, you make yourself at home in one of the alcoves near that large radiator. It's the warmest place here. As soon as we get the boxes, I'll leave you two alone. Try not to scandalize Poe."

Poe, the cat, gave a single unimpressed blink.

When Ivar returned, he placed the boxes on the table and removed his jacket, tossing it on the chair. Holly blinked. He was wearing his park ranger uniform: dark green pants, a pressed shirt, and a badge gleaming faintly in the lamplight. Somehow, it made him look both official and wildly out of place among the dusty books and curling pages.

"I didn't realize your vacation was over," she said, guilt flickering across her face. "I didn't mean to pull you away from work."

"If saving the forest isn't part of my job, then I'm doing something wrong."

Her lips curved. "I suppose there's something to be said for men in uniform."

He raised an eyebrow. "Only something?"

"Don't push your luck, Ranger."

Mim's voice floated from behind the shelves. "Children, please. Some of us are still within earshot."

Holly bit back a laugh as Ivar sat beside her. A stack of leather-bound journals waited beside them, their covers cracked, edges flaked with age, each marked with the same looping initials: **C.H.**

Holly traced them lightly with her finger. "Cornelius Hale."

"Who's that?" Ivar asked, leaning in close.

"Henry learned his name from some of the old-timers. According to Henry, some of those who leave our world are drawn to Yule veins, whether they realize it or not. He said, for some, it's like living near a pulse, a steady rhythm, like a second heartbeat."

Ivar tilted his head. "That's poetic."

"Yes, I suppose it is. These people are called Keepers."

"So, what do they keep? The land safe? Or your secret?"

"Good question," Holly said half to herself. "Henry said it was because they were drawn to the magic veins, but keeping our secret makes sense too, because they've left and they're trusted to keep it. Oh dear, this might be a wild-goose chase."

Somewhere in the distance, Mim hummed tunelessly while shelving books.

"Come on, Kringle," Ivar said gently. "Don't give up. We've got the journals, and a name that matches the initials. Let's see what he has to say."

Mim's voice drifted from the next aisle. "And remember, darlings—whispering only counts as quiet if you're not blushing while you do it!"

Holly shot Ivar a mortified look, which he answered with a grin.

"Come on," he said. "Start reading."

Mim's chatter faded as Holly opened the brittle first page. The journal began with notes about the house Cornelius and his wife were building. The garden they were planning. How many goats they wanted. Holly followed their progress through the first few years. The next journal started with plans for a maple orchard.

They kept reading entries about weather and crops, and occasionally some local gossip. Then, one passage caused them both to pause.

March 24, 1884

This morning brought word that the parcel of land adjoining my northern boundary is to be sold. I have no intention of expanding as my maple orchard keeps me well enough occupied, but some curiosity is compelling me to see it. Tomorrow, I will walk the ridge to see the property for myself.

Holly turned to Ivar. "This is it," she whispered. "This has to be the land."

"Keep reading," he said.

March 25, 1884

It is a strange piece of ground, dense with pine and hemlock, the kind of forest that muffles a man's own footsteps. The path down is steep and half-hidden, as though the land does not wish to be approached. Yet the moment I crossed its boundary, a stillness took hold of me. The air was close and cool, carrying no birdsong, only the faint hum of unseen life beneath the soil.

The trees here stand differently than in my own woods. They are older perhaps, but not in decay. Straight and tall, their bark pale and smooth as carved ash. I felt as though I had entered a chapel built not by man's hands but by time itself. And there, in the hollow of the valley, the ground curved inward, forming a great bowl where the mist seemed to rest like breath upon a mirror. The snow, though fresh that morning, had melted there, and the earth gave off a subtle warmth, like embers hidden deep beneath the ash.

I did not see the source of that warmth, nor could I name what stirred in me as I stood there. It was not fear, nor was it comfort, but a knowing. The land, I think, wished to be left in peace, but it also wished to be kept. Not cleared, not built upon. Simply watched over.

I left before dusk, yet the image of

that hollow has not left me. There is purpose in that soil, older than I can reckon. I will make an offer on the land at once. Whatever it is that sleeps beneath those roots, it is not meant for men to disturb. Better it rests under the hand of one who will protect it, than fall to those who would see only timber and profit.

I do not yet understand why, but I know this: I am meant to protect it.

Ivar leaned back in his chair, eyes still fixed on the page. For a long moment he didn't move. "He bought the land to protect something he couldn't even name." His voice was quiet, almost reverent. "Do you think he ever saw the tree?"

"I'm not sure. If he'd been cho-sen..." She hesitated, about to start a conversation that would change Ivar's life yet again. "Then yes, he would have seen it."

"I'm sorry. You lost me there. Cho-sen?"

She nodded slowly. "Henry found some information about a 'Heart Tree' and a 'Root of Light' dating back to pre-Santa times. It's what we now call the Yule Tree." She pulled up the picture Henry had sent.

The drawing filled the center of the yellowing paper. It wasn't a realistic tree but a symbolic one: its trunk rising straight and true, its roots and branches mirrored in perfect symmetry. The limbs curved into spirals that hinted at runes, and tiny marks like stars or embers dot-ted the spaces between, as if light had been translated into pattern.

The shape suggested an evergreen by its branches, which were tiered and tall and edged with needle-like strokes. But it was too symmetrical to be anything found in nature. It wasn't a tree so much as the idea of one: life and light rendered as geometry.

Ivar rubbed the back of his neck. "Until I met you, I would have thought this was too strange to be true; now, nothing surprises me." He pulled his field notebook from his coat pocket and flipped it open. Between maps and trail notes were sketches of the same tree. "I've been doodling that tree since I was a kid. I thought I had made it up. But clearly there's more to it. Obviously, that tree's more than just the epicenter of a worldwide magical power source."

He focused on the picture again, pointing to the margins. "I mean, look at this. The light sleeps beneath the roots. It wakes when the world forgets. What does that even mean?"

"Where does it say that?"

"Right where I'm pointing." He tapped on her phone.

Holly didn't know what to say.

"Great. Now what?" Ivar asked.

"I can't read that. To me, it's lines and markings."

Holly watched his color drain, leaving him ashen . The drawings, the prose, had peeled back something he wasn't ready to face.

"I need some air," he murmured, rising from the chair like the building was on fire.

"Wait for me."

"I'll meet you outside."

Holly took a few quick photos of the pages before straightening the journals carefully, almost afraid to disturb what they'd just uncovered.

Whatever she'd been afraid to say before, it couldn't wait any longer. She'd finish what she started and tell him everything.

YULE THE MAN

<u>Ivar</u>

The silence between them was loaded as they walked the wooded trail to Ivar's cabin. Al thumped his tail, excited they were home, but didn't bother to move from the rug.

Ivar went straight to the fireplace, bracing his hands on the mantel. "Tell me what's going on, Holly. Because those drawings..." He turned to her, eyes searching. "You knew something before we went there."

"You're right." Her voice was quiet, trembling slightly, which did nothing to calm him down. "I've been trying to find the right words and the right moment."

He exhaled, dragging his hand through his hair. "Do your best, please, because I'm starting to freak out."

He busied himself stacking wood in the hearth even though there was no fire. Anything to keep his hands busy with something familiar, something real.

"Henry's research found references to a legend about the Yule Tree and its... Guardian." She paused, as if giving him time to brace himself for what was to come next.

"Don't say it, Holly, please."

"But it's the truth. You're the Guardian."

He gave a shaky laugh that caught half-way through. "Guardian? Come on."

"I know how it sounds," she said quickly, stepping closer. "But listen. The story says the Yule Tree only reveals itself when the world starts to lose balance—when people forget what connection means. And when it does, it calls someone to protect it. Not a Kringle, not a Santa. Someone rooted to the land."

He was flooded with confusion and disbelief, not to mention panic. But there was something else, too. A recognition he wasn't ready to accept.

"Ivar, that's why you saw the tree as a child," she continued softly. "Why you've been sketching it your whole life. You were chosen long before you understood what it meant."

"I still don't understand what it means." He pressed his palm against his chest, wanting to steady his heartbeat. "And chosen? I'm not anyone special. I'm a failed game designer and a park ranger in a small town in Vermont that no one's heard of." His voice cracked with fear.

"You're wrong," she argued. "You listen when others talk. You see what others miss. You make people feel safe without even realizing it. That's not ordinary, Ivar. That's rare. That's why the forest trusts you. Why friends and family trust you." Her eyes found his. "Why I trust you."

He turned away, staring out the frosted window toward the line of trees beyond the pond. The world outside was still and glimmering, as if it too was waiting for his acceptance.

She came beside him. "My family's job is to keep joy and hope alive. Maybe yours is to guard where it grows."

He was silent for a long time. Finally, he whispered, "I thought I was managing okay when I learned that magic was real. Now you're telling me that I didn't just stumble upon it by accident all those years ago, but that it chose me?"

Holly nodded. "Exactly."

He ran a hand through his hair again, the motion slower this time. "You realize how crazy this sounds?"

"I do." She stepped closer, laying her hands on his chest, his heart. "But I also know you've felt it. The searching. The pull the day we found it. The cardinals. The poinsettia you healed. The perfect tree you created."

"The sounds of the forest," he continued. "The dreams." Guardian, the wind had whispered.

He looked down at his hands, calloused from years of fieldwork and trail repair. Hands that built, fixed, held. Hands that, apparently, were meant to protect something he didn't understand.

California had felt like failure—walking away from a career he'd built, from a life he thought he wanted. The betrayal, the exhaustion, the noise of it all had stripped him bare. He'd come back here to disappear, not to be found.

He'd sought peace. Solitude. But the woods were never truly silent. There was always a hum beneath everything, the faint pulse of life under the snow. He'd always thought it was wind or water.

Now he wasn't so sure.

That was a lie. He was sure.

Maybe belief isn't something you find, he thought. Maybe it's something that finds you when you stop running from it.

And today was the day he stopped running.

He closed his eyes, sending his acceptance out into the forest.

The wind blew, rattling his windows and stirring up snow. Message received. He'd been acknowledged. Welcomed.

What exactly this all meant was still unclear, but with each passing second he became a little lighter, like he was moving toward something he hadn't dared believe in for a long time—himself.

When he opened his eyes, Holly was waiting patiently, her expression steady.

He opened his arms, and she stepped into them. The embrace wasn't just comfort—it was connection. Two lives, two callings, two halves of the same promise.

Two entwined branches in the shape of a heart.

He longed to kiss her as if to seal their destiny, but he knew, he knew, this was not their moment.

"What happens now, Kringle?"

"We finish the mission, Ranger. We protect the Yule Tree."

He'd tried to sleep. He really had. However, the tree sketch and the word Guardian appeared whenever he shut his eyes. Even Al had tired of his tossing and turning and left for the living room with a heavy sigh.

He rolled over and reached for his phone. The one person who would understand.

Ivar: Can't sleep. You?
Holly: Zzzzz. Joking. Don't know why you'd have any problems sleeping. Just a regular old day.
Ivar: If weird days become more frequent than regular days, does that make regular days weird?
Holly: [mind-blowing emoji]
(pause)
Ivar: Thanks for being there for me.
Holly: Always. We're in this together.
Ivar: You're just saying that because a magical tree zapped us with electricity.
Holly: That certainly helped.
Ivar: Next time, let's aim for fewer life-altering revelations and more cookies.

Holly: Deal. Sweet dreams, Ranger.
Ivar: Only if you're in them, Kringle.

15
days until
Christmas Eve

BE-LEAF IN MAGIC

<u>Holly</u>

The noon sun glinted off the snow, bright enough to make Holly squint as she helped Liv tie the last garland to the gazebo rail. Her fingers were numb, her cheeks flushed, and yet there was a deep satisfaction in seeing the square come together.

Tomorrow was the last day of the carnival, and Liv wanted the gazebo to look spectacular as it would host a full day of choirs and bands before the festivities ended with a town-wide dance.

She reached for the last garland, laughing under her breath as Liv adjusted it for the third time. "Perfectionist tendencies run in your family, you know."

Liv arched an eyebrow. "You're one to talk."

Before Holly could answer, a familiar voice carried across the square.

"Holly!"

She turned. Chad stood at the base of the gazebo, his expression sharp enough to cut through ice.

"Hello, Chad," she said carefully. "Enjoying the festival?"

"Hardly." He took a few measured steps closer, boots crunching on the packed snow. "You must be proud of yourself."

"Proud?"

"Rowan called the town hall today. She's blocking the development. She says you and your friends convinced her to keep the land as it is. Now she's even talking of moving here."

"We never told her not to develop the land," Liv said, moving beside Holly.

"Not in so many words." His hand shook as he ran it through his hair. "I don't know who you are, but you're obviously not an investor. So tell me, Holly, who are you?"

"I'm someone who believes this forest deserves to stay whole."

Chad let out a humorless laugh. "Whole? You think these people will thank you when the jobs don't come? When nothing changes?"

"They don't want change if it destroys what's already good."

He started to go, then paused. The edge in his voice broke for the first time. "Rowan's all I've got left. You should've stayed out of it." Without another glance, he disappeared down the snowy street, swallowed by shadow and distance.

Holly exhaled shakily, realizing her hands were clenched. Liv placed an arm around her. "Don't let him upset you."

Suddenly, Ivar appeared behind them, out of breath, with Al trotting at his side.

"Ivar? What on earth? Did you run here?" Liv asked.

He nodded, still catching his breath.

"Why?"

"The wind... I heard... never mind. Are you guys okay?"

Holly nodded. "That was Chad. Rowan said no to the development."

"Well, that's that then," Liv said, though her tone was more bewildered than triumphant. "Not gonna lie, I thought it would take more than that. Anyway, I've gotta get back to the inn. Enjoy your peaceful victory. Oh, and Ivar? You might want to start jogging again."

Liv shrieked and ran down the gazebo stairs as a snowball narrowly missed her hat.

Ivar threw another snowball for Al to chase before stepping into the gazebo beside Holly. They stood together in silence, staring down the empty path where Chad had disappeared.

"I know our plan was to change their minds," Holly said finally, "but this feels... anticlimactic. I guess I'm a sucker for a Hollywood ending, but it's weird for something to end without fireworks. Why am I not happy it's over?"

A gust of wind whipped through the town square, knocking over signs and blowing snow.

Al let out a low whine, ears twitch-ing.

Ivar scratched the dog's head and reached for Holly's hand. "Because it's not," he said quietly.

Ivar

By late afternoon, the clouds had moved in and the snow had start-ed. Ivar checked the weather. Heavy snowfall was predicted, but not a storm. Just winter in Ver-mont. He normally liked days like this, but Ivar couldn't settle.

He paced between his desk and the window, boots creaking against the floorboards. Al lay nearby, ears pricked, tail twitching restlessly. Every few seconds, he gave a low, uneasy whine.

"I know," Ivar muttered. "I feel it too."

He tried to focus on the reports scattered across his desk—trail maintenance logs, updated permit lists—but the words blurred. The forest felt wrong today. Not loud, not dangerous... off.

Al rose suddenly, padding to the window, nose pressed against the glass. A soft growl vibrated in his throat.

"What is it, buddy?" Ivar joined him, scanning the tree line.

He reached for his jacket, the hair on the back of his neck prickling when the door burst open and Chad barged in.

Ivar didn't know what to expect from the man.

"Ivar, thank goodness you're here."

The man's tone wasn't angry this time. It was frayed and coated with fear.

"What's wrong?"

"It's Rowan. We were fighting over the land, and we both said some horrible things. She took the car and drove off. Now she's not answering her phone. I'm worried something happened to her."

Ivar's heart dropped. "When did she leave?"

"Two hours ago. Maybe more. I thought she'd cool off and come back, but—" His voice cracked.

"How do you know she's not simply having dinner in the next town over?"

"She doesn't have her wallet. It's on the kitchen table. And she hates driving in the snow."

Ivar grabbed the phone and called Carla. "We need a search and rescue party organized. Now."

"Stay by your phone," Ivar said, moving with determination around the office, assembling gear.

"I'm coming too."

"That's not a good idea."

"I don't care. She's my sister."

Within thirty minutes, the whole town had gathered in the square. The carnival lights were still on, but the cheer had been replaced with silent determination and concern.

"Our trained search and rescue volunteers have their assignments. Everyone else, it's too risky to send you into the forest. If you're going to search, I want you in groups of three or four. Check the back roads, the main roads in and out of town, anywhere she might've pulled off. I don't want anyone else to go missing. Keep your radios on channel three. Liv and Mim are coordinating at the town hall. So if you can't get through on your radio, call them there."

"Ivar," Holly called, catching him as he headed to his snowmobile. "Listen to me for one minute."

He stopped walking.

"I'll go up. Into the air," she whispered.

"It's too risky. There's too much snow, and it's dark."

"We go out in the snow all the time."

"Yeah, but don't you have routes? Coordinates?"

"Not when we go out for fun."

"But would you go out for fun in this? I can't let you do that. It would be flying blind."

"I can't stay here and do nothing. I'll go with you."

Ivar, about to agree, was interrupted.

"I'm going with him," Chad said, walking over to them. "She's my sister. I'm not sitting here waiting for news."

For a moment, no one spoke. Then Ivar nodded once. "Fine." He pulled Holly aside. "Stay with Liv in the office. I could use your help in coordinating the volunteers. And Al, stay with Holly."

She leaned in and hugged him. He was hoping for another kiss on the cheek. Instead, she whispered, "Listen to the forest, Guardian."

For a heartbeat, everything else fell away except for the echo of her words and the weight of what they meant.

When she stepped back, he could only nod. Then, with his pulse thudding in time with the wind through the trees, he returned to his snowmobile.

"Put this on while I hook up the rescue sled," he said to Chad, tilting his head toward a snowmobile suit.

"What about you?"

"I'm used to it," Ivar said. "I'll be plenty warm."

With the sled attached, he zipped up his parka and pulled on his mitts. "Is there somewhere she might go? A favorite trail?"

There was a pause while Chad considered this. "Betty used to take us swimming at a pond," Chad said. "I haven't been there since I was ten. Rowan would have been three at the time, but Betty took her there each summer. Just the other day she told me how much she loved it." He gave a short, uneasy laugh. "I used to hate it. The forest made my skin crawl. It still does."

Ivar glanced at him. "But you're coming anyway?"

"She's my sister."

They set off in the direction of the Hale property. "What did this pond look like? Do you remember anything specific?"

"Nothing really. But Rowan pointed to the road you take to the trail head the other day as we drove past. It's a bit east of the house."

Ivar knew where he meant. He'd been in that part of the forest before—just not often, and not recently. It wasn't a popular hiking route, maybe because it ran too close to the Hale house.

Twenty minutes later, the snowmobile's headlight swept across a small clearing and caught the gleam of Rowan's car.

Ivar had barely cut the engine when Chad jumped off and sprinted toward it.

"It's empty!" he shouted, running back to the snowmobile. "Come on. Let's go!"

"Wait. I need to think." Ivar killed the engine. The snow was tapering off, and the wind was dying down. Still, the infrequently used trail would be hard to follow.

"What are you doing?" Chad yelled, his panic reverberating inside Ivar's helmet.

"Trust me, I need a minute." There was something in his voice. Authority? Whatever it was, it made Chad sit still.

Meanwhile, Ivar's mind was spinning—too many paths, too many sounds, all blending together into static. He needed it clear.

He gripped the handlebars tighter and took a deep breath. Sometimes it's not magic, Holly had said. It's observation.

Fine, he'd observe.

He shut out the noise, even Chad's breathing through the Bluetooth headset, and listened. Really listened.

Images, sensations, memories began forming a cohesive message.

The day they'd found the tree. They hadn't forced their way forward; they'd followed.

I'm listening. He pushed the thought out into the night.

And the forest answered.

It began as a pulse beneath the snow, subtle as a heartbeat. The trail appeared, as clear as daylight, cutting through the trees where there'd been only darkness.

"Hold on," he said.

He turned on the snowmobile, gunning the engine, and the snowmobile launched forward. The path unfolded before him, bending and widening as the forest itself guided them through. He knew every turn, every hidden rock, every low branch before it came.

While one part of his brain remained locked on the trail, another part fractured open—falling, spinning, expanding.

It was like slipping through time.

The darkness burst into color, flashing in wild succession: flocks of birds rising over lakes; fish twisting through sunlit water; flowers blooming and wilting in fast motion; trees budding, greening, turning gold, then bare again. He felt the tremor of roots under ice, the deep groan of rivers, the flicker of firelight under snow.

He saw himself—a boy standing beneath the Yule Tree, light spilling over him like a golden dawn. Then, as a man holding Holly's hand in his, their hearts beating as one, and then, it changed again. A flash of blue. A small boy, lost in the forest. Chad.

Another flash. Rowan, stumbling through the snow, her scarf whipping in the wind.

"There!" Ivar shouted. "She's up ahead!"

"How do you—"

But Ivar was already accelerating, eyes locked on the invisible path only he could see.

The forest opened, and as they tore through the clearing, the hum beneath the ground rose like a wild, ancient song and guided him straight to her.

A flash of red reached him through the darkness, followed by movement at the base of a slope. He cut the engine, and quiet rushed in like a tide.

"There!"

They ran, boots sinking into knee-deep snow. Ivar reached her first. Rowan was curled against a fallen log. She'd made a partial shelter out of pine boughs, but was shivering, and her face was almost as white as the snow.

"Rowan!" Chad's voice cracked, half shout, half prayer.

"Hey," Ivar said softly, dropping to his knees beside her. "You're okay now. We've got you."

Her eyes fluttered open, unfocused for a moment before she saw Chad. "You came," she whispered.

"Of course I came. You're my sister," he said, breathless, his voice rough. He kneeled beside her, pulling her into his arms. "You could've frozen out here, Ro."

She let out a trembling laugh. "I told you I'd be fine. I just needed to think."

"Next time," Chad said, holding her tighter, "think somewhere warm."

Ivar stood, scanning the trees as the pulse that had guided him faded into a slow, steady rhythm.

He glanced down at the siblings. Chad murmured something that made Rowan smile through her tears. Their relief was palpable. Chad still had his fear, but it was nothing compared to the love for his sister.

When Rowan was steady enough to stand, Ivar helped her to her feet. She leaned against her brother, weak but smiling.

"Let's get you home," Ivar said. "I'm going to carry you to the snowmobile and wrap you up warmly in the rescue sled. It'll be a bit bumpy, but I'll radio for someone to meet us at the trailhead."

They made their way back to the snowmobile in silence.

With Rowan secured and warm, Ivar started the engine, glancing once more into the dark forest. The pines stood still, sentinel and ancient. And for a moment, he thought he saw a faint green glow deep among the trees, like a breath of the aurora.

He turned back to the trail, the rumble of the machine carrying them toward Winterwood. Back toward home.

HOLLY-DAY BLUES

<u>Holly</u>

While she waited for Ivar to get back from the hospital, Holly searched his cupboards. He'd texted that Rowan was fine and would be home soon, so she busied herself with finding something to make for dinner.

Al walked into the kitchen and stretched out across the floor.

"Don't get your hopes up," she told the dog. "My culinary skills are limited."

She opened the fridge, relieved to find eggs and cheese. "It will be either omelets or scrambled eggs, depending on how they turn out. Sound good, Al?"

Al's tail thumped on the floor. She'd wait a few more minutes before starting so the food would be hot for Ivar's arrival.

With the land issue resolved, the Yule Tree would be safe. And yet, beneath the relief, her thoughts tumbled, because it was time for her to return home.

Christmas Eve was only two weeks away. She should be at NED, overseeing logistics, scheduling sleigh routes, reviewing last-minute toy reports. She'd built her whole career—her life—on keeping Christmas running like clockwork.

But now, in Ivar's kitchen, with a fire crackling and a dog at her feet, she decided to step back, take a breath, and let someone else run the show. Just this year—she wasn't quitting; she'd never do that—but she needed a break. She didn't want the season to feel like a deadline anymore.

And she didn't want to spend the season without Ivar. They'd been through too much, their connection too strong, for her to leave at what she considered the beginning of them.

Confident in her decision, she pulled out her phone and dialed.

Rita picked up on the second ring. "Boss? Everything all right? Are you still in Vermont, or are you home?"

Home. Ivar was home. "I'm still in Vermont, and I'm staying here for Christmas."

There was a pause. "Staying? But the Christmas Eve run—"

"I know. That's why I'm calling. Nicola and Finn are ready. It's time they took the route. They can each do half."

"You're serious?" Rita's voice dropped to a whisper, as if someone might overhear. "Holly Kringle is taking a vacation?"

"Don't sound so horrified," Holly teased. "It's for professional development. For them and for me."

"But you're not quitting, are you? Giving up on your dream of Chief Executive Santa?"

"Oh, heck no. I'm simply changing my strategy."

Rita let out a breath that turned into a laugh. "Well, thank goodness."

"I'm letting you know first because you'll need to start planning for this. Just give me a day or two to notify my father. Then you're free to tell the troops."

"Will do," Rita said in a tone that was practically a salute. "Have a happy holiday. You can tell me about him when you get back."

"Rita!"

"Ha! I knew it. Enjoy!"

"You too." She was about to hang up when she added, "Rita... I wouldn't feel comfortable doing this if it weren't for you. Merry Christmas."

Holly smiled as she ended the call. For the first time in years, Christmas wasn't a checklist. It was an open door.

She was about to block the Christmas Eve countdown alert her father's office sent out every day, then stopped. This year, she wouldn't see it as a reminder of all she had to do. She'd see it as a tradition she'd been part of her whole life.

"Let's get cracking and make dinner," she said to Al, laughing at her own joke.

The cheese had just been added to the eggs when Ivar returned. He walked in, kicked off his boots, hung up his coat, gave Al a scratch, and then walked over to Holly at the stove, wrapping his arms around her. "What a night," he said. "Rowan is safe, and I get to come home to you."

"I'm making you dinner."

"Smells great."

"It's just eggs."

"Dinner is a gift, and it's the thought that counts."

She laughed, plating the eggs right as the toaster popped. And as they sat together in the cozy little cabin in the woods, Holly had never been happier.

They'd just started eating when her phone rang. "It's Henry. I'd better take it."

"Ciao, Hol. I'm in Italy. I took your advice, and you were right. I got a lot of great information."

"Henry, you're on speakerphone. Ivar's here too."

"Ivar? The Guardian?"

Ivar started choking on a mouthful of eggs.

"Henry. Come on," Holly admonished.

"Sorry, this is all very exciting. It's like meeting a legend."

This time Ivar nearly launched his mouthful of eggs across the room.

"What's going on?" Henry asked.

"Hold on," Holly said, muting the phone. "Are you okay?" she asked, half laughing, giving Ivar a few whacks on the back. "I'm getting you a glass of water."

"You don't find it funny? Someone from the Santa family calling me a legend?"

"Huh. I guess that is kind of funny."

"Thank you. That's all I'm asking."

She unmuted the phone. "Hey, Henry, we're back."

"Okay. The reason I'm calling—" There was a pause as Henry flipped through the pages of his notebook. "According to what I've pieced together, the Yule Tree is very particular about when it appears. It chooses when and to whom."

"So it chose to show itself to us," Holly said.

"It's not that simple," Henry said. "And honestly, I don't quite know what this means."

Something in his tone caused a little ball of fear to form. "So, what did you find?"

"Most of the old texts say that only the Guardian can truly see it—like, really see it, not just sense the Yule veins beneath it or see some light. The Tree only reveals itself to the one it trusts. Everyone else walks past it without realizing what they're standing beside."

"But Henry, I saw it."

"Did you really, or did you just sense it?"

"We both saw it. We both felt it. We... never mind."

There was a long pause. "Holly. It could be important."

Ivar reached across the table and squeezed her hand. "We held hands, and the power of the Yule Tree traveled through us, connecting us to each other and to the forest," he told Henry. "I don't know how else to explain it."

"Holy smokes." Henry's voice was barely a whisper. "Hol, this is huge. Why didn't you tell me this before? You guys are basically rewriting our understanding of history in real time. These tomes I'm finding—no one's looked at them in decades, centuries even."

"A bit dramatic, no?"

"Well, yes, but that's because it is. What you're telling me isn't in the texts. But I did read—where is it?—hang on one second." He shuffled more books around. "I think it's in here. Ah, yes. Here it is. I found one passage that describes a rare exception. I hadn't paid it

much attention, but that was a mistake."

"An exception?" she and Ivar asked
simultaneously.

"Yeah. According to the text, when
both connection and giving fall
out of balance at the same time,
the Yule Tree calls not one, but
two—the Guardian and the Giver."

Holly sat up straighter. "The Giver?"

"Loosely translated, yes," Henry
said. "The Guardian protects the
land's heart—keeps us grounded
and reminds us how interconnected we all are with nature, each other, the elements, the world. The
Giver restores the balance of spirit.
Through generosity and kindness,
we are reminded of why it all matters. But when both forget their
purpose, when the Guardian can
no longer connect, and the Giver forgets how to give with her

heart..." He took a deep breath. "They need each other to heal."

Holly's throat tightened as she turned to Ivar. "The Yule Tree called us both."

"Looks that way," Henry said softly. "It must be rare, as I only found mention of it once. But the notes say that when they find each other, their light spreads twice as far."

"So, how do we know when things are back in balance?" Ivar asked.

"I haven't come across that yet," Henry said. "But I'll keep looking."

"You do that," Holly said. Although was that what she really wanted? More legends and ancient truths?

Henry hung up. A dense silence filled the room, so thick it was practically suffocating.

"Sooo," Ivar said after a minute passed. "That was your brother."

"Yup. He really geeks out over stuff like this." Holly picked at her eggs, no longer hungry. For a moment, all she heard was the faint hum of the refrigerator and Al's soft snoring.

"So," she said finally, "it's not only that you're the Guardian. It's that the Tree called us both because..." She couldn't bring herself to finish the sentence.

"Because things fell out of balance," Ivar said gently.

"No. Not things. Us. You and me." She stood, pacing around the room.

"It might not only be about us, but also what we represent."

"Ivar, that is not helping. I do not need more pressure while I figure this out."

"Hol," he began gently. "The Yule Tree wasn't wrong about me—and yes, that sentence did leave my mouth. But kidding aside, I've been withdrawn since returning from California. But then you came into my life, and I'm living again."

She leaned on the kitchen counter, allowing the tears to flow freely. "My whole life has been about giving. It's all I ever wanted to do. It's my job, and I worked tirelessly to be the best, only to discover that a tree judged me and found me lacking." She half laughed, half sobbed. "How can a Santa fail at the only requirement in the job description?"

His chair scraped on the floor as he pushed it back, joining her, his arms wrapping around her. He pulled her close, and she leaned into him, his embrace like a sponge, absorbing her pain. The miracle of it almost caused her to weep, for at her darkest moment, she was not alone.

Because the truth had hit her, and it was hard to bear: a Santa who had turned giving into a job. Who treated Christmas as nothing more than a to-do list, full of spreadsheets and production quotas.

Holly clung to him, her lifeboat, as her words poured out. "How do I fix this, Ivar? I've changed, I know I have. With you, I've rediscovered joy and fun. I even phoned Rita and told her I was taking Christmas off this year because I want to spend it here with you."

His happiness hit her like a wave. "You don't have to do that. I can come with you, provided that's allowed."

"You're so sweet, and yes, it's allowed, but I wanted to enjoy Christmas and not have it be a checklist." She leaned into him. "Oh gosh. That says it all, doesn't it? Darn that tree. I guess it's two for two."

"It would appear that way." He leaned past her, grabbing a box of tissues. "Here."

"Thanks."

"Just be gentle. Those were friends of mine once."

Holly snorted out a laugh through her tears.

A silence stretched out then, and she reached for his hands, loving the way his rough fingers wrapped around her smaller ones. She leaned against his chest, listening to his heart beat in sync with hers—two hearts beating as one. Guardian and Giver. Chosen to fix the balance.

Chosen.

She stepped back. A snowball of panic formed, and it started rolling downhill. "Think about all that's happened since we held hands in front of the Yule Tree."

"Okay."

"What do you think it means?"

"Guardian-and-Giver-wise, or you-and-me-wise?"

"Do you think we can separate them?"

"I do."

"Then you and me."

"Easy. It means we were meant to be together."

"But aren't you worried that the amazing connection we have was created only for the purpose of 'restoring the balance?'" she asked, mocking Henry's voice. "What if it's not real?"

He squeezed her hands tight. "There's not a single cell in my body that questions whether what we have is real. My heart knows it, my brain knows it, even the very tips of my fingers know it."

"I'm not so sure." Her voice was barely more than a whisper.

Her head dropped against his chest. "I'm going back to the inn. I need some time alone."

"Whatever you need, for as long as it takes. I'll be here when you're ready." He was trying to be strong for her, but she heard the heartache in his voice, felt his pain pulse through her, and it twisted her heart into knots.

She slid into her coat and boots and walked out softly into the night, leaving her heart behind.

Back at the inn, she lay in bed, staring at the ceiling while tears ran down her cheeks. She loved Ivar, but how could she ever be sure it was real, that they weren't just pawns in some weird cosmic game. There was so much to process, so much to consider. She'd come to Winterwood to assess Yule lines. How did it get so complicated?

"I should have stayed at NED. This is why I don't take vacations."

Her broom fell over. "Don't act all offended. You took us to the tree. If anyone should be mad, it's me at you." She leaned out of bed to prop up the broom. As soon as she touched it, she heard La Befana's voice. "When the time comes, it will guide you to the truth your heart has forgotten." She scoffed. "Why does everyone have to speak so cryptically?"

We don't choose where the magic leads us. We choose whether to follow it.

The light sleeps beneath the roots. It wakes when the world forgets.

"I want answers!"

The fire flared up, the desk rattled, and her window burst open. She watched helplessly as her broom flew out of the room like it had somewhere better to be. And with a last gust of wind, her window shut, and the fire returned to normal.

"Now what?" she wondered, rubbing her temples.

Beside her, her phone pinged, and she didn't have to look to know it was Ivar. She automatically reached for it, stopped, then picked it up anyway.

Ivar: So... the Carnival Dance. You coming?

She chuckled, wiping her tears away.

Holly: That depends. Are you asking as a chaperone or as a date?
Ivar: Definitely not a chaperone.
Holly: Then I'll think about it.
Ivar: I'll pick you up at seven.
Holly: You're very confident.
Ivar: Not confidence. Faith.
(pause)
Holly: See you at seven, Ranger.

14
days until
Christmas Eve

HOLLY NOT-SO-JOLLY

<u>Holly</u>

Holly lay in bed listening to the radiator pipes banging in the walls the way her heart banged against her chest.

Sleep had been restless. Every time she closed her eyes, she pictured the Yule Tree, felt the pulse that had connected them, and wondered if their bond was fate or choice. She'd yet to figure it out.

Eventually, she forced herself to get out of bed. Her body hurt from heartache. Never had she experienced such deep emotional pain. It would take everything she had to get through the day. So, she decided she would simply move through the world and see what happened. There was no job, no project, no plan, no mission, nothing. A completely unfamiliar way of being.

And as for Ivar and the dance? She would go. It meant something. She didn't yet know what, but she hoped it wasn't goodbye.

Downstairs, the inn was already alive with morning chatter. Liv spotted her immediately and hurried over, holding a comically large mug.

"I know how much you like your coffee," Liv said, proudly presenting it. The mug read, Full of Holiday Spirit (and Coffee).

Holly attempted a laugh, hoping it sounded genuine. "You have no idea how perfect this is."

"Oh, I think I do," Liv said, filling it generously. "Watching you consume caffeine is basically a sport."

Holly smiled into her cup. "You always know what people need," she said softly.

Liv shrugged. "That's just small-town intuition. Speaking of which—a little bird told me you're going to the dance tonight."

"With your brother," Holly admitted.

"Good," Liv said. "You should. You two... it's like you found something most people spend years looking for." She tilted her head. "But you'll be heading home soon, right?"

Holly hesitated. "Yes. Eventually."

"Are you going to do the long-distance thing? You know, I don't even know where you're from?"

"A bit north. But I'm not worried about the distance. I have a lot of air miles." That was the least of her worries with Ivar.

"Well, good. Because I've never seen two people connect faster than you two. It was like," she made a jagged chopping gesture with her hand, "lightning."

"It certainly was."

"Well, I better throw another pot on. See you later."

Holly grabbed a pastry and returned to her room, bucket of coffee in hand. The first thing she did was take a picture of the mug and send it to Rita.

Then, before she could lose her nerve, she called her parents and let them know about Christmas. She wasn't sure if she'd be here in Winterwood, because if she couldn't get past the reason for their connection, what future did they have?

Luckily, Henry had filled them in on the whole Giver / Guardian thing, so they understood. Then they just acted like parents. Was she eating right? Sleeping? Staying warm? She answered them honestly. She was healthier. Her watch rarely beeped, she was sleeping better, and while she hadn't quit coffee, she'd at least quit espressos.

As soon as she hung up, Holly switched it to silent in anticipation of a flurry of messages from cousins and siblings. And if Ivar texted, she'd know.

With hours remaining until the dance, she bundled up and stepped into the crisp air, following the sound of carolers through the square. She bought a few small gifts. Maple candy for Liv's boys, and for Liv, a reindeer that pooped jellybeans (if only). She laughed out loud when she came across a dog bandana that read, "Snack Guardian," and bought it immediately.

The day was sunny, the town beautiful, the people friendly, but without Ivar, nothing felt the same. Reminders of him were everywhere.

She was sitting on a bench, staring at the Christmas tree Ivar had somehow manifested when she saw Rowan and Chad enter the Maple Mug.

George gave them a wave as he walked by. Winterwood had definitely warmed up to them.

Something stirred in her mind, like puzzle pieces clicking into place, though she couldn't quite see the full picture yet. Chad. Rowan. Cornelius. Keepers. The Guardian. The Yule Tree. Connection.

If anyone had become disconnected from the land, and from each other, it was Chad and Rowan.

What if this was about more than preserving the land? The Hales had been tied to it for generations. What if...

Her thoughts spun faster now. It sounded wild, maybe even ridiculous, but what if this journey wasn't only about protecting the forest? What if it was also about healing the family bound to it and helping them find their way back to each other?

She texted Ivar, but there was no response. He was working and was likely busy, but she didn't want to wait.

Without a plan, she entered the Maple Mug and found their table.

"Can I join you for a minute?"

"Of course." Rowan smiled. Chad nodded.

"How are you feeling, Rowan?"

"Much better. I can't believe I got lost. I thought I'd always know my way to the pond, but it's been so long since I've been here. I guess I forgot."

"That's kind of what I wanted to talk to you both about."

"The trail?"

"No," Holly said gently. "The land and your absence from it. Your property is... special. This might sound strange, but hear me out. One of your relatives, Cornelius Hale, discovered how special it was and vowed to protect it. I don't know how to explain this exactly, but Cornelius could feel the land. It has a rhythm, and I think that sensitivity to it runs in your family."

Chad scoffed. "Who do you and Ivar think you are?"

"What do you mean?" Rowan asked.

"She's trying to trick you, the way Ivar tried to trick me last night," Chad said, though the color had drained from his face.

"Trick you?"

"Yes." He leaned across the table toward his sister. "He kept trying to convince me that the forest was warning me of danger."

"What on earth are you talking about?" Rowan asked.

Chad exhaled, his voice quieting. "He knew about something that happened when I was a kid. Something no one should have known. I was playing in the forest, and something scared me. Ivar said the forest was protecting me from danger. Not trying to frighten me. It sounds insane, but he described everything right down to the color of my boots."

"So someone lives in our forest?" Rowan asked.

"No," Holly said softly. "It was the forest."

Rowan frowned. "I still don't under-stand."

"Start by reading Cornelius Hale's journals," Holly said. "After that, either Ivar or I can answer your questions. Our families are connected, and one day, I'd like to tell you the full story."

"Okay, I guess," Rowan said, who was clearly still processing.

"There's one more thing," Holly added. "And maybe this is just small-town intuition"—she smiled, borrowing Liv's phrase—"but you both belong here. Chad, you mocked that hometown feeling because you never really had it. Now's your chance. Stay in Winterwood for a while. Explore your family's past. Reconnect with the town, and especially with each other. Maybe that's the project that brings you closer."

"You know, you and Ivar are something else," Chad said to her, but there was no anger in his voice.

"Oh, you have no idea." Holly stood, pushing in her chair.

Rowan reached for her hand. "Thank you for this."

Holly squeezed Rowan's hand back, hoping she'd made a difference. "You're welcome."

As she turned to leave, she used a bit of Santa magic so that, when Rowan and Chad glanced down at their lattes, the foam now held the faint outline of the Yule Tree. She hoped it would leave them in wonder and somehow serve as a reminder of what mattered most.

When she stepped through the inn's front door, she was feeling a little lighter. She hadn't solved Rowan and Chad's problems, but maybe she'd given them a nudge in the right direction.

To her surprise, Liv was waiting with a mischievous grin and an armful of sweaters.

"Holly Kringle," she declared, "you cannot attend the Winterwood Carnival Dance without proper Christmas attire."

"What do you mean?"

"I mean, Christmas sweaters are a must tonight. It's tradition. So, you're borrowing one of these."

Holly looked over the selection. One was embellished with a moose tangled in lights, another with a grinning Santa that said Sleigh All Day. She couldn't picture herself in either. If she had to wear a novelty shirt, she at least wanted one Ivar would appreciate.

"Oh," she said suddenly. "I've got it."

"You have one?" Liv asked.

"I do." Or she would by tonight.

"You think you know a person," Liv teased.

Holly raced up to her room and texted Rita.

Holly: I need a favor. How quickly can you get me a Christmas sweater?
Rita: For you?
Holly: Yes.
Rita: Where's the real Holly Kringle and what have you done with her?
Holly: Very funny.
Rita: I think you know how fast I can get it for you. You wrote the procedure.
Holly: Perfect. Here's what I want it to say.

Holly finished texting Rita, her smile lingering.

The sweater would say it all.

The answer had come to her as she left the cafe, thinking about wonder and what mattered most. The past few weeks with Ivar had been nothing but wonder. And when it came to what mattered most, it was love.

Ivar was her other half. Steady where she overthought. Patient where she pushed. She needed him. Wanted him. Loved him.

The fear that fate had chosen for her would probably always linger, but she could live with that. What she couldn't live without was him.

THE HOLLY AND THE IVAR

<u>Holly</u>

Holly stood at the mirror, chuckling at her sweater for the hundredth time. It was perfect, and she couldn't wait for him to see it.

Finally, the inn's grandfather clock chimed seven. Her heart skipped as she slipped on her shoes, did up her jacket, and stepped into the hallway. Liv's warm greeting drifted upstairs, followed by Ivar's deep voice.

Taking a deep breath, she walked to the stairs and paused.

Ivar stood in the lobby below, talking quietly with Liv. The warm light caught in his hair, turning it gold at the edges. A dark green sweater poked out from under his jacket, and in his hand, her broom.

Her breath caught in her throat. Not only did he have her broom, he'd put a tiny hat and scarf on it.

As if sensing her presence, he looked up.

"Hi," she said, descending the stairs.

"Hi."

Liv glanced between them, then made herself scarce.

"Sorry I missed your text earlier. The only place that had my Christmas sweater in stock was in Montreal, and I forgot to toss a phone charger in the truck. As soon as I saw the design online, I knew it would make you laugh, so I had to go get it."

"You drove to Montreal?"

"I'd do anything for you. Driving to Canada was nothing."

"Ivar…" was all she managed, but her eyes said the rest. Her throat tightened, and an ache of tenderness spread through her and wrapped around her heart. He'd crossed a border for her—literally.

"I'm assuming you didn't take my broom," she teased after a moment. "So, why do you have it?

"Actually," Ivar said, holding it out to her, "it found me. I woke up this morning and there it was, leaning against my front door."

Holly took it gently. "It has a mind of its own sometimes."

"I've learned that." His eyes never left hers.

As she stared into those stunning blue eyes, understanding dawned. She'd asked for answers, and she'd gotten one. La Befana had said that when the time came, it would guide her to the truth. And it had done. He was standing right in front of her. But she'd already figured that out.

Ivar moved closer. "You asked me once if I believed in fate," he said, his voice low. "It occurred to me that you might have been worried about us even then." His eyes were serious, searching hers. "But I don't think we're here because of fate. Fate implies a lack of personal control."

Holly nodded, waiting for him to continue.

"I think our situation has more to do with destiny," he went on. "Destiny sets us on a path, but we still have personal agency. We make choices. We take actions." His hand covered hers on the broom handle. "There are stories galore about unfulfilled destinies. But that's not our story."

"No?" she whispered.

"No," he said firmly. "Our destiny is fulfilled because we made it happen. It didn't happen to us."

"So you don't think… what we fee l… it's not just because of the Yule Tree?"

"The Yule Tree may have brought us together," he said, his thumb brushing over her knuckles. "But every moment since has been our choice. Every laugh, every conversation, every text message. That was us, Holly. Not magic."

She looked down at their joined hands on the broom, then back up at his face.

Yes. He was right. She could now see how every decision, every hesitation, every step they'd taken had led them here. Not because of some magical decree, but because of who they were and what they chose, again and again.

The magic hadn't bound them; it had simply cleared the path. The rest they'd done themselves. They weren't surrendering to love. They were choosing it.

"You're right," she said softly. "We're more than Guardian and Giver."

"Much more," he agreed. "We're Kringle and Ranger. Holly and Ivar."

She carefully set the broom against the wall and took his hand properly in hers.

"In that case, Ranger, I believe you promised me a dance."

His smile lit his whole face. "So I did, Kringle. So I did. Oh, but we can't forget the broom. I agreed to let it chaperone."

Holly couldn't believe how the town hall had been transformed into a winter wonderland. Evergreen garlands draped from exposed beams, fairy lights twinkled like captured stars, and red velvet bows adorned every pillar. The band—five locals with fiddles, a guitar, piano, and an upright bass—tuned their instruments on the small stage while the dance caller, an elderly man named Walter with suspenders and a white beard that rivaled her grandfather's, arranged his notes.

Holly stood at the edge of the polished wooden floor, watching as townspeople streamed in. Liv bustled by with a tray of cider cups, winking as she passed. Tess and Marty hung additional wreaths near the refreshments table, playfully arguing about symmetry.

"Ready?" Ivar asked, his hand warm against the small of her back.

"For contra dancing?" Holly laughed.

"First, our sweater reveal. I'll show you mine if you show me yours."

"Okay, on the count of one, two, three." They unzipped their jackets.

"Oh, my gosh," Holly cried. "I love it." Ivar was wearing a green sweater with a Christmas tree on it. I'm Pining for You.

"I think yours takes top prize," Ivar said. "All I Want for Christmas is Yule. That might be the most appropriate Christmas sweater I've ever seen."

"I don't know," Holly said. "They're both perfect. And if you stand on my left, technically our sweaters read, Yule Tree."

"There, see? We are perfect for each other. Hey, can we wear these when I meet your parents? A little Guardian / Giver humor to break the ice."

Bursting with joy, Holly threw her arms around him. He caught her easily, laughing as he lifted her off the ground and spun her in a circle.

He set her down just as the first notes from the fiddle cut through the room, silencing the crowd. Walter's booming voice followed: "Ladies and gentlemen, find your partners! Form two lines facing each other."

Ivar gave a mock bow and extended his arm toward her. "Shall we?"

For twenty minutes, the dance continued—switching partners, forming stars and circles, weaving between lines. Holly enjoyed the magic of it: not Santa magic, but the simple human magic of community, of joy shared and multiplied.

When the music finally paused for a break, Holly was breathless and glowing. The room buzzed with chatter and laughter. Liv circulated with trays of cookies, while Tess handed out cups of her special winter brew.

"That," Holly declared, accepting a cup of water from Ivar, "was not what I expected."

"I hope in a good way," he said, leaning against the wall beside her.

The band struck up a slower melody, sweet and nostalgic. Couples drifted to the center of the floor, arms encircling waists and shoulders.

Ivar offered his hand. "May I?"

Holly placed her palm in his. "I thought you'd never ask."

He led her to a quieter corner of the dance floor, where the crowd had thinned. His hand settled on her waist, warm and sure. Unlike the energetic chaos of the contra dance, the waltz allowed them to move as one, steps aligned in perfect time.

"You know," he murmured, "for someone who claims she doesn't dance, you move like you've done this forever."

"Maybe it's my partner," she replied, looking up at him.

His eyes never left hers as they turned slowly. In the soft glow of the lights, with snowflakes drifting past the windows, they drifted to the edge of the dance floor, where the music was softer. Holly noticed Ivar's gaze shift upward.

Following his eyes, she saw it: a sprig of mistletoe, tied with a red ribbon, hanging from the beam above them.

Their steps slowed until they were barely moving, just swaying together in the corner of the room.

Their eyes met beneath the mistletoe, the music fading to a distant hum. Holly's breath caught as Ivar's hand gently cupped her cheek.

"I've been waiting for this since the moment you called me Ranger," he whispered.

"That long?" she murmured, her fingers resting lightly on his chest.

He leaned down, and as their lips met, the world disappeared around them. It was like standing in the eye of a hurricane—utterly still while everything else spun. That same energy she'd felt beneath the Yule Tree pulsed between them, coursing through every point where they touched. It flowed through her veins, between her cells, until she was sure they'd become pure energy, lifting them higher and higher.

Colors burst behind her closed eyelids—silver and gold, emerald and azure—like the forest and sky had merged inside them. For a moment that stretched into eternity, Holly wasn't sure where she ended and Ivar began, their connection complete and perfect.

Then, gradually, she became aware of the music again, of the solid floor beneath her feet, of

Ivar's arms holding her steady. They were still on the dance floor, surrounded by spinning couples, as if nothing extraordinary had happened.

Their lips parted, foreheads leaning against one another.

"Wow," Ivar breathed.

"Yeah," she whispered back. "You're a heck of a kisser, Ranger."

His laugh was soft. "It takes two."

The moment was interrupted when the door burst open, a blast of cold air sweeping in. George stood framed in the doorway, his face illuminated by a strange, shifting light from outside.

"Everyone, you've got to come see this!" he shouted. "It's the Northern Lights. I've never seen anything like it!"

People rushed toward the exit, exclamations of wonder rising as they spilled onto the street. The music faltered as even the band members set down their instruments to investigate.

"You don't want to see the lights?" Holly asked, noticing Ivar hadn't moved.

He shook his head, his eyes never leaving hers. "No. I'm exactly where I want to be." His fingers traced her cheek with impossible tenderness. "Besides, nothing in the universe could ever outshine what I have right here."

He leaned in and kissed her again, slow and sweet, while outside the lights shimmered and danced across the winter sky, their colors reflected in the snow like thousands of fallen stars.

Music from the dance played in Holly's head along with memories of their kiss as she lay in bed waiting for Ivar to text. She didn't have to wait long.

Ivar: You make a habit of kissing people under government-issued mistletoe, Kringle?
Holly: Only those with excellent sweaters and questionable dance skills.
Ivar: Ouch. You didn't complain during the Winterwood Reel.
Holly: I was too dizzy. Also, that was your fault.
Ivar: Sure. Blame the ranger.
Holly: Always.
(pause)

Ivar: You know, when I walked you back to the inn, I could sense the change. The balance.

Holly: Me too. Everything felt... right.

Ivar: And so do you... in my arms.

Holly: Careful, Ranger. You're one text away from getting added to my nice list.

Ivar: What happens when I get there?

Holly: You stay there. Permanently.

(pause)

Ivar: I love you, Kringle.

Holly: Took you long enough.

Ivar: How did you know? Observation or magic?

Holly: A Kringle never gives up her secrets.

(pause)

Holly: I love you too, Ranger.

SANTA GROUP CHAT

Remember, team—sleigh safe out there!

Let's keep it merry and bright AND on schedule!

Try not to mix up Vancouver, BC and Vancouver, WA this year, Martin!

Sleigh the night, everyone!

Okay Santas—check your lists, check your GPS, and for the love of cocoa, hydrate.

EPILOGUE: THE CLAUSE EFFECT

<u>Chris Kringle</u>

Christmas Eve, and Winterwood was buzzing with the kind of cheerful chaos that meant the season had fully arrived. The Town Hall Kids' Breakfast with Santa was in full swing: carols playing, cocoa steaming, and at least two dozen children vibrating with sugar and belief.

The only problem? Santa was sick.

Liv was near panic when Holly and Ivar arrived. "The suit's ready, but there's no one to fill it," Liv said, wringing her hands. "The kids will be heartbroken."

Holly looked at the empty chair on the stage, the red suit hanging behind it, and smiled slowly. "I might know someone."

Ten minutes later, the doors swung open.

"Ho-ho-ho!"

Every head turned. The children squealed. Parents blinked in astonishment.

Santa had arrived with a big bag of presents hanging from a... broomstick?

The suit fit perfectly—red velvet trimmed in white, the beard full and glossy, the boots gleaming. But it wasn't just the costume. This Santa had presence. The air shimmered faintly, the scent of peppermint and pine growing stronger with each step.

"Good morning, Winterwood!" Santa boomed in a voice so jolly it could've powered the sleigh itself. "I hear there are some very good boys and girls here today!"

The room erupted in cheers.

"Santa" sat in the big chair as the line of children formed. Each child climbed onto the red velvet lap, whispering wishes in tiny, eager voices. And somehow—impossibly—Santa already knew their names.

"Hello, Daisy. How's your new puppy, Sprinkles?"

"Connor! I hear you've been helping your mom shovel the driveway. Very impressive!"

"Emmy, those mittens look wonderful. Did you knit them yourself?"

The children's faces glowed, and parents snapped photos through tears and laughter. And when each child left, they carried a small wrapped gift—exactly the thing they'd asked for in their letters.

Behind the crowd, Ivar leaned against the doorway, arms crossed, brow furrowed. Holly was in the suit, but he could hear that Santa voice she'd done in his cabin. Most unnerving.

Did no one else notice that the five-foot-four woman had a voice like James Earl Jones?

Liv stood beside him, taking pictures.

"Am I the only one who finds that weird?" Ivar asked.

"Finds what weird?"

"How Holly can—" he stopped. "Can I see the pictures you just took?"

"Sure."

He scrolled through them. While he saw Holly, the rest of the room saw Santa.

He handed the phone back to his sister.

"Did you know about these new gifts?" Liv asked him. "These aren't the ones we ordered. In fact, the order never went through. The money's still in the town's account."

"I think Holly said her family was making a donation."

"Oh. That explains it. A Christmas miracle."

"Uh-huh," Ivar murmured.

Then Santa looked straight at him and winked.

"Oh, and we have a very special helper today!" the deep, booming voice announced. "A certain ranger who's been very good this year."

The crowd laughed and turned toward Ivar, who groaned softly. "You've got to be kidding me."

"Come on up here, Ranger Nilsen!" Santa called, beckoning him with a white-gloved hand.

"I'm good right here," Ivar said.

"Don't make me put you on the naughty list," Santa said sternly, the twinkle unmistakable.

Liv nudged him. "Ivar, the kids are waiting."

Begrudgingly, he walked over to Santa. Santa patted his knee. Ivar sat on Santa's knee.

The eyes behind the spectacles sparkled. Ivar leaned in close. "You're enjoying this, aren't you?"

"Immensely," Santa whispered back, but in her own, Holly voice.

And then, in a perfect, booming Santa voice, she said, "And look what we have for Ranger Ivar—a new pair of binoculars. Ho-ho-ho!" Santa roared, and the kids shrieked with delight.

Ivar took the binoculars. "You're impossible," he whispered.

Santa leaned closer as the next child climbed up. "And you love it."

When the breakfast ended, the children waved and cheered as Santa disappeared out the side door in a swirl of snow. Moments later, Holly reappeared, cheeks flushed, hair slightly mussed.

Ivar was waiting for her by the door, arms folded but a smile tugging at his mouth.

"Very convincing," he said. "And what if I told you I was beginning to like that Santa voice?"

Holly tilted her head back, laughing.

Ivar laughed too, slipping his arm around her shoulders, joining the crowd for breakfast. The bells from the church tower chimed in the distance, and the sound rolled across Winterwood like pure joy.

The End

ABOUT JANET KOOPS

Janet Koops is a Canadian living in Colorado. A former librarian, Janet is a happily married empty-nester who writes full-time from her home just east of the Rocky Mountains. When she is not writing, she can typically be found hiking with her Alaskan Husky or working on a DIY reno project. Janet is a hopeless romantic who loves writing about complex women, their emotional journeys, and the healing power of love.

Connect with Janet!
janetkoops.com
Goodreads: janetkoops
BookBub: @janetkoops1

Instagram: @janet_koops
Pinterest: Author Janet Koops
janet@janetkoops.com

For a complete list of Janet's books, please visit
https://janetkoops.com

www.ingramcontent.com/pod-product-compliance
Lightning Source LLC
Chambersburg PA
CBHW022015300726
48970CB00003B/899